Faro Buys Himself
a One-Way Ticket
to Trouble . . .

The door at the front of the caboose swung open. Faro turned his head, and the detective kicked the Reid out of his hand, then lashed out with his fist. His short, powerful arms propelled his knuckles like a pile driver into Faro's jaw, sprawling him back across the caboose. Then the detective snatched up the satchel and made a leap for the rear door. He was going to jump!

Faro rolled toward the door and caught the detective's leg just as he was going out. In a moment they both lay in a pile in the open doorway. Kicking, punching, and gouging, they rolled out onto the landing at the back of the caboose. Faro lashed out with his foot and caught his opponent between the legs. The detective roared out in pain and let go of the satchel. Faro rose to his feet. "I think it's about time I punched your ticket," he said. He raised his foot and gave the detective a hard kick in the midsection. A quick yelp of surprise, and then the detective's body struck the ground beside the tracks and rolled out of sight down the embankment . . .

Westerns by Zeke Masters

Published by POCKET BOOKS

Most Pocket Books are available at special quantity discounts for bulk purchases for sales promotions, premiums or fund raising. Special books or book excerpts can also be created to fit specific needs.

For details write the office of the Vice President of Special Markets, Pocket Books, 1230 Avenue of the Americas, New York, New York 10020.

#31

A ZEKE
MASTERS
WESTERN

UP FOR GRABS

P

PUBLISHED BY POCKET BOOKS NEW YORK

Another *Original* publication of POCKET BOOKS

POCKET BOOKS, a division of Simon & Schuster, Inc.
1230 Avenue of the Americas, New York, N.Y. 10020

Copyright © 1983 by Pocket Books, a division of
Simon & Schuster, Inc.

ISBN: 0-671-49307-8

First Pocket Books printing November, 1983

10 9 8 7 6 5 4 3 2 1

POCKET and colophon are registered trademarks
of Simon & Schuster, Inc.

Printed in the U.S.A.

UP FOR GRABS

Chapter One

Louisa took the cheroot from Faro, inhaled deeply, and then returned it to him. She let the smoke curl gracefully up from her lips into her nostrils in the manner of her countrymen, then smiled at him when she realized he was watching her. But his eyes dwelled more on the luxurious curves of her body than on the way in which she smoked.

"You don't come here to see me so much anymore, *chéri*," Louisa said. "Maybe I start to think you don't love me anymore." Her voice was soft and marvelously sensual, with a smooth French accent which in itself was an aid to romance. But Louisa Fontaine had other qualities as well which had drawn him to the brothel where she worked and the bed where she practiced her trade.

"I don't get back to St. Louis much nowadays," Faro admitted. "But that doesn't mean I could ever forget you, Louisa. You've got something that no other woman I've ever met has."

"You mean I *don't* have something the other women have," Louisa giggled, glancing down along the length of her naked body.

"That's definitely it," Faro agreed, letting his eyes travel the same pathway. Now, after enjoying more than three hours of Louisa's intimate company, his eyes still savored everything they saw. He lightly caressed the nub at the base of her abdomen where her right leg should have been, knowing it gave her an odd sort of delight. She laid her head back and closed her eyes, smiling contentedly.

Fifteen years before when Faro Blake first found himself alone with Louisa, sitting on the edge of her bed while she removed her artificial limb, he had been appalled at the idea of making love to a woman with only one leg. But it had taken Louisa only a few minutes to show him what unimagined sexual advantages her infirmity could provide. Now, on the rare occasions when Faro visited Madame Jessica's in St. Louis, he never considered investing his time and money with any woman but Louisa Fontaine.

The smile slowly dissolved from Louisa's features and a look of quiet sadness replaced it. "If you wait so long to come back and see me again," she told Faro, "maybe you won't find me here at Madame's the next time."

Faro raised up onto one elbow and looked at her in alarm. "Don't tell me you're quitting the business," he said. "Hell, woman. You're an institution here in St. Louis. The city just wouldn't be the same without you!"

"The years pass, *chéri*. In another few months, I will be thirty-eight years old. It is long enough to do this kind of thing."

8

"But you've still got a body that would put the rest of these young twits to shame," he protested. Somehow he just couldn't imagine Madame Jessica's or St. Louis without Louisa there.

"Time takes it all away though, my dear friend Faro," Louisa told him wistfully. "Sometimes I can tell the weather now by the pains in my stump. And last week I had a young man make a request which shows how it could become for me if I stayed too long. When we were in bed together, he asked me if he could call me 'mama.'"

Faro grinned, though the message beneath what she was telling him was hardly humorous.

"I have saved my money, and soon I go back to my own country," Louisa told him. "I have lived here half my life, but France is still my home. I will marry a Frenchman and grow old where I belong."

There was a yearning quality to their embrace, and for a time it seemed as if Louisa simply needed to feel the arms of a good friend holding her tightly.

It was all changing, Faro thought with a surge of nostalgia. Hickock was dead and Jesse James was dead. The buffalo had been all but annihilated, and the scattered survivors of the once proud western Indian tribes were now dying lingering deaths on stark reservations. The best of the whores were hanging up their golden garters for good.

They drifted off to sleep together, still wrapped tightly in their embrace, but the nap was a short one. Faro roused when he heard heavy footsteps in the hall outside. Some instinct alerted him to impending danger. He was halfway across the room, heading toward his clothes and the Reid's Knuckleduster derringer in his jacket, when the door burst open and three men stomped in. Faro stopped, realizing how senseless it would be to go for the gun now.

"This here is real cozy, Blake," Gravedigger Smith announced. "Real goddamn cozy!" He threw a sneer at Faro, then let his eyes wander over to leer at Louisa's naked form. She stared back at him defiantly, refusing to acknowledge his intrusion even by pulling the sheet up over her body. "But the thing that occurs to me," Smith went on, "is that if you've got the cash to lay up with one of the most expensive whores in the city, then you should be able to come up with the money you owe me!"

Faro found the mere act of looking at the man repulsive. Bosephus "Gravedigger" Smith was a squirrely runt of a man with front teeth like a beaver's and the shifty stare of a possum caught sucking eggs in the henhouse. On more than one occasion, Faro had pondered what a pleasure it would be to test how much of that face he could destroy with one blow from his right fist, but he knew that the two grizzly bears Smith kept with him would never permit such a thing. Both of them looked as if they would rather break a man's bones than sit down at their mama's table for a home cooked meal.

"I told you I'd come up with the thousand dollars to pay for those markers," Faro told him. "If there's one thing I don't do, it's welsh on my gambling debts."

"All I've got is your word for that, Blake," Smith replied. "And right now your word don't seem to be worth much more than spit on a hot griddle."

"Look, Smith! You know how little action there is in St. Louis right now, what with the big clean-up campaign and all. Hell, your place is the only one in the city that's got any gambling going on, and that's just because the chief of police is married to your sister. How do you expect me to get the money if I can't practice my trade?"

"I ain't here to tell you how to get it, tinhorn," Smith snarled. "Hell, steal it from little old ladies on the street if you have to. What I am telling you is that three days have passed since you signed those markers in my place, and that goddamn thousand dollars is due! Bad things happen to sonsabitches that fuck with me in this town."

As he was talking, Smith strolled over to the side of the bed so he could gaze directly down at Louisa's prone form. She bore his stares with icy indifference. But when he reached out to catch one of her nipples between his thumb and forefinger and gave it a twist which brought a sudden look of pain to Louisa's features, it was more than Faro could tolerate.

He launched himself forward across the room, but the grizzlies intercepted him before he could get his hands on their boss. When one of them locked his paw on Faro's left arm, Faro spun and hit him square in the midsection with his right fist. It was like punching a piece of boiler steel. The second bodyguard caught Faro's right arm before he could swing again, then brought his knee up and crashed it into Faro's stomach. The blow knocked the wind out of him and he crumpled forward in their grasps.

Smith's two enforcers were damned good at what they did. It took them only a couple of minutes to inflict a score of painful bruises and cuts in various places on Faro's body. When they finished, he lay in a disheveled pile on the floor, not particularly inclined to move or get up. Raising his head slightly, he caught sight of a set of legs and feet directly in front of him, and by the immaculate white of the patent leather spats, he knew they belonged to Smith.

"This is nothing, Blake, nothing compared to what you're going to get if you don't come up with that money by this time tomorrow," Smith told him, kicking him in the chest for emphasis.

After the three men were gone, Louisa helped Faro drag himself onto the bed. Then she strapped on her artificial leg, pulled on a wrapper and went out for a pan of water and some cloths. When she returned, she began bathing his assorted wounds.

"You didn't tell me you had trouble with that one," she chided him gently.

"I've been dodging his bunch for two days," Faro said. "I guess I should have figured they might spot me if I came here. I'm sorry I brought this trouble to you."

"It's not that *chéri,*" Louisa told him. "The Madame, she has an understanding with him and he would never hurt me badly here in this place. But he is a wicked man. It is a bad thing to owe him money and not to pay."

"I know that," he replied, "but there's not one hell of a lot I seem to be able to do about it. Right now gambling seems to be a dead art in this town, and Smith's people are watching the ways out of town so there's not much chance of going somewhere else and coming up with the cash. I've even thought about just killing the little turd and being done with him, but with his brother-in-law being the chief of police and all . . ."

"I must give you the money to pay the Gravedigger," she told him with a gentle smile. "Maybe it is the only way to save your life."

"The money you've saved to go home?" Faro asked. "No, ma'am! There's no way in hell I'd use your money to line the pockets of that son of a bitch."

"But you must do it," Louisa protested. "It is the only way."

"I'd strangle that buck-toothed little fart with my bare hands before I'd do that," Faro vowed. "And I can't say that it would be such a chore, either. Especially not after today."

Faro swirled the double shot of brandy around in the snifter, gazing at the delicate tracings the liquor made on the inside of the glass and savoring the aroma. It wasn't very practical to spend a portion of his last ten dollars in the world on what amounted to only one good mouthful of strong drink, but somehow in this desperate situation he craved the luxury of expensive liquor. The brandy stung when it hit the cuts on the inside of his mouth, but it was a healing sort of sting. Louisa had done a pretty good job patching him up and the marks on his face hardly showed in the dim barroom light.

He took another sip of brandy and tried not to think about the times he had bought this stuff by the case and poured it around for friends and strangers alike.

Years ago, St. Louis had been different. In the late fifties when he had first traveled there as a wide-eyed youth on a Mississippi steamboat with his gambler father, St. Louis had been a hell-for-leather frontier town, busting at the seams with all manner of iniquity and good times. If his daddy was still alive, old A. B. Blake sure wouldn't know the place these days, Faro reflected. All the same vices still flourished, but big-city graft had taken over. Now the main intent was no longer to provide a freewheeling good time for all comers, but to dip as deeply as possible into a man's pockets and leave him on the skids.

Maybe it had been a mistake to come back, but he had wanted to see the river and the big boats again. He felt some craving to travel back through time, to recall the days when he had apprenticed in his trade under the expert tutelage of his father and old Doc Prentiss, the craftiest con man ever to make a sucker feel happy to be bilked. But he should have known better. The Civil War had rung the death knell for the steamboat trade. It wasn't the same anymore, and all this journey seemed to be accomplishing was to tarnish those fine old memories. It would have been better to remember it as it was.

The small, elegant bar off the lobby of the Hotel New Brunswick was practically empty now. Once it had been the watering hole for riverboat captains, pilots and fancy gamblers riding the crest of Lady Luck, but those breeds of men were nearly extinct now. These days when successful men gathered here, they were more likely to be talking about the tides of the commodities market than the shifts in the river channel following the spring runoffs. Times changed.

Faro emptied the brandy from his glass and set it down on the long, polished mahogany bar. Then he raised his head and stared at his own image in the mirror behind the neatly tiered rows of liquor bottles. He mustered a smile, strictly for his own benefit, and felt better for it. Things had been a hell of a lot worse for him at other times during his life. What he needed to do now was haul his freight out of St. Louis. But first there was the matter of Gravedigger Smith, and that was proving to be a thorny problem.

In a minute the bartender came toward him carrying a brandy bottle. "Thanks, but I'll take a pass this time," Faro told him.

The bartender poured a measure of liquor into the snifter anyway, explaining, "It's on the gentleman at the far end of the bar."

Faro raised his glass and saluted his benefactor before drinking. With that encouragement, the man started down the bar toward him. Faro was not in any particular mood for company, but he figured that if he could drink a stranger's liquor, he could share a few minutes of conversation with him as well.

"Excuse me if I'm disturbing you," the man said, "but I judge you to be a rather interesting gentleman. Perhaps it's the way you're dressed."

Faro was wearing his customary gambler's togs—black broadcloth suit and vest, frilled white shirt, silk tie and black calfskin boots. As soon as he arrived in St. Louis he realized that this was hardly the fashion of the day in the city, but these were the clothes in which he felt most comfortable.

"My name is Anthony Winchell," the man said, extending his hand as he offered the introduction.

"Pleased to meet you," Faro replied, accepting the handshake. "I'm Faro Blake." Winchell was a man in his early forties, immaculately groomed, and dressed in a neat, nondescript business suit. It was difficult for Faro to get much of an impression of him beneath his smooth manners and superficial friendliness. But Faro was sure of one thing from the start. He wanted something.

"The last time I saw a man dressed as you are, it was down by the docks about ten years after the war," Winchell said. "Two roughnecks were harassing a young woman of obvious breeding, and when this gentleman tried to interfere, they began to threaten him. In the wink of an eye both the roughnecks were dead, shot through the heart, and the man was apologizing to the young woman for exposing her to such a scene of violence. He was a professional gambler from Nevada named Duke Sims, if I recall correctly."

"I've met Sims," Faro admitted. "He's quick-tempered and fast as a snake, but you must have seen him on one of his better days. He doesn't always have such good cause when he takes a notion to kill a man."

"Might I assume that you're in the same line of work, Mr. Blake?" Winchell asked.

"That would depend on who you are and why you're asking," Faro told him. "Ever since I got to St. Louis, all I've been hearing about is the big crackdown on gambling and other vices here. It seems like gamblers aren't such a popular breed in these parts nowadays."

"It's an election year," Winchell said with a chuckle, explaining the current purge. "But you don't have to worry about me in that regard. I am second vice president of the Fidelity Trust Bank here in St. Louis and I have no involvement whatever in politics. I came over here simply out of curiosity."

Faro considered the statement a moment, then looked his companion in the eye and asked, "Why do I doubt that, Winchell?"

A surprised look came onto Winchell's face, but he was quick to replace it with one of amusement. "Very astute of you, Mr. Blake." He smiled. "But then, I suppose sharp instincts are necessary in your profession. The fact is that I was trying to gauge you to see if you might be suitable for a job I have in mind. And I am impressed."

"Well, it's a hell of a load off my mind to know I impressed you, Winchell," Faro said with vague irritation. He figured a man was only entitled to so much bullshit for the price of a double-shot of brandy, and Winchell had just about used up his money's worth. "But banking's not my line," he added.

"Maybe I've used poor judgment here and perhaps I've gone about this in the wrong way," Winchell conceded. "You probably have good reason to be suspicious of my approach. But I've been looking for a particular type of man for a particular job that has nothing to do with working in a bank. It is a short-term assignment that pays well and involves a one-way trip to New Orleans."

That did interest Faro. "How well is 'well'?" he asked.

Winchell sensed that his hook was set, and he started getting cagey. He smiled shrewdly at Faro and said, "Such matters can be negotiated, but the main thing for me to know now is whether or not you could be available immediately to do the job."

"If everything was right, I could be available," Faro told him. "But I'd have to know exactly what I was taking on beforehand, and my services wouldn't come cheap."

Winchell produced a card from the pocket of his vest and handed it to Faro. "The address of the bank is on here, Mr. Blake. Could you come around my office at ten tomorrow and discuss the details with me? I dislike transacting business in public places."

"I can be there," Faro promised.

"Splendid," Winchell said, shaking his hand again. "I'm sure this is going to work out fine for both of us. I'll see you tomorrow."

After the banker had gone, Faro nursed the remaining brandy in his glass for a long time, pondering what had just occurred. The way Winchell had approached him was at least strange, and more like downright suspicious. But what could it hurt to go hear him out at the bank tomorrow? If it seemed like trouble he could always turn the job down, and if it did happen to work out, it might provide him with a quick solution to his recent problems.

In celebration of the prospects, Faro splurged on another brandy, then left as the bar began to fill up with its evening clientele. Louisa had taken the evening off from her duties so they could have dinner, and with any luck, their final night together would continue until morning.

Chapter Two

Louisa feigned sleep as Faro dressed and prepared to leave her room. The best kind of good-bye was none at all. But as he paused in the doorway and glanced back a final time before going out, he noticed a single tear rolling down her cheek.

It was a fine thing when a whore cried for a man, Faro thought as he went down the broad main stairway of Madame Jessica's and out the front door. Though he rarely saw her anymore, Faro knew he would miss Louisa too once she was gone for good. But she would do well. When she returned to France, she could manufacture any past for herself that she wished, and with her charm and good looks, she would have no trouble finding a good man. And once the fellow found himself in bed with her for the first time, he would fully realize what a rare treasure had come his way.

Faro's attitude was much improved this morning. The prospects of clearing things up with Gravedigger and leaving St. Louis probably had a lot to do with it, but he couldn't discount the effects of a night of satisfactions with a good woman, either. Despite his earlier apprehensions, he had a feeling that this job with Winchell would be to his liking and that soon he would be on his way to New Orleans. Conditions were certain to be better there.

The Fidelity Trust Bank was an impressive-looking place, a somber assemblage of marble, granite and glass in the midst of the burgeoning financial district of St. Louis. Faro strolled in the front door as if he owned controlling interest in the place, ignoring the suspicious looks of the guards. After inquiring with a clerk at a desk to one side, he was guided toward the rear of the building and ushered into a plush, paneled office.

Winchell sat behind a huge oak desk, looking utterly at home in his stuffy dominion. His tone was less conciliatory today. He seemed more in control of the situation, and though he still greeted Faro with the same smooth courtesy, there was also an edge of dominance in his attitude.

"Please have a seat, Mr. Blake," Winchell offered, pointing to a seat across from his desk. The chair put Faro's eye level slightly lower than Winchell's. "Drink?" the banker offered.

"It's a little early," Faro said. "Why don't we just skip the formalities and get right to business?"

"Fine, fine," Winchell agreed, leaning back in his chair and linking his fingers across his midsection in a studied pose of calm. "Here's the situation. As soon as arrangements can be made, one of the clerks from this bank will depart by train for New Orleans carrying this satchel of important bank documents and investment records." He reached down beside him on the floor and lifted a plain-looking canvas satchel up onto the desk. It was open wide enough for Faro to glimpse the bundles of papers inside.

"In New Orleans," Winchell continued, "the satchel will be turned over to the captain of a ship, a trusted associate of mine, and will be transported to an affiliate bank in London. Once the documents are on board the ship, they will be safe, but the assignment I have for you is to accompany the clerk and make sure the satchel reaches New Orleans safely. The trip should take no more than three days by train, and I have in mind a payment of one thousand dollars. I'm sure you will have no problem figuring out what to do with an amount that size."

Faro read plenty into the shrewd look on the banker's face. He seemed to be playing with more hole cards than Faro had given him credit for during their last meeting. Faro had to wonder if it was mere coincidence his fee was set at the same amount he owed to Gravedigger Smith.

"The job sounds simple enough," Faro admitted. "That is, from what you've told me so far. But I do have a question. Why me? Why a stranger that you know nothing about except that I have a taste for expensive brandy in hotel bars?"

"You struck me as right for the job," Winchell explained vaguely. "And you do need the money, don't you?"

"I've got a pretty good notion that you know already how much I need it," Faro said. "But that doesn't mean I'll take the job. The only thing that's going to keep me from walking out that door in about thirty seconds is some straight talk. Let's start with Gravedigger Smith."

The banker's eyebrows turned down with concern,

and he said in a rather confidential tone, "I'm always hesitant to admit to any association with men of Smith's type. But the fact is that he did recommend you to me for the job. He was having you followed yesterday, and our meeting in the New Brunswick Bar was hardly a coincidence."

"So he 'recommended' me, huh?" Faro scoffed. "That's old Gravedigger, all right. Always looking out for the well-being of his fellow man."

"I really didn't want to bring his name into this because I knew it would make you even more suspicious. We both know that Mr. Smith couldn't care less what happens to you, but he does want the money you owe him. He plans to be at the depot tomorrow and collect his payment right after I give it to you."

"It all makes sense so far," Faro conceded. "It stinks like donkey droppings, but it makes sense. But that still doesn't explain why me."

"In order to explain that, I'm going to have to take you into my confidence, Mr. Blake," Winchell said. "What is discussed here can never be mentioned beyond this office. Is that agreeable to you?"

Faro nodded with some reluctance.

"This satchel contains the records of a number of the bank's transactions over the past six months which might be considered, er, questionable. Were they to see these, the state bank examiners might ask some very embarrassing questions about Fidelity Trust's overseas investments and involvements, and that is the reason that this transfer is being handled in such an unusual manner. If this satchel were to fall into the hands of our competitors, they would make sure an investigation was conducted. Are you beginning to understand?"

Faro nodded again.

"I wanted to select a man to go along who looked like practically anything but a guard, and yet could think fast in difficult situations and wasn't afraid to be heavy-handed if the necessity arose. You seem to fit that description, and it strikes me that you couldn't have survived very long in your profession unless you were good at taking care of yourself in a crisis. Is that true, Mr. Blake?"

"I've managed so far," Faro told him.

"You will not be breaking the law," the banker continued, "and we have no concrete reason to expect any trouble. The chances are good that the most serious problem you'll have on the trip is boredom."

"It couldn't be much worse than sitting around this damn town waiting for Gravedigger to show me how he came by that monicker," Faro admitted. "But we still have one thing to work out between us before I say 'yes.' It's about the fee."

Winchell stiffened. "A thousand dollars seems more than generous," he bristled. "It will solve your problems with Smith, and your train fare to New Orleans will also be paid, of course."

"But once I hit New Orleans," Faro explained, "I'd prefer to land with both feet under me. And I can't ignore the possibility that there could be some danger along the way. Another thousand dollars in the pot might convince me that it's worthwhile."

"Absolutely not!" Winchell replied. "It's out of the question."

"Well that settles that," Faro said, rising to his feet. "I have an appointment to keep with a ferret-faced piece of outhouse slime, and I'm sure you're going to be busy combing the barrooms for another man of dubious integrity. So I'll bid you good day."

Winchell waited until Faro's hand was on the door

knob before offering up his compromise. "Fifteen hundred, and not a dime more," he growled.

Turning with a grin, Faro asked, "When and where?"

"Be at the main depot at 2 P.M. tomorrow. I'll have your money and your ticket waiting. You will not meet your traveling companion until the train is under way, but the two of you will have adjoining compartments."

"When this is over, Winchell," Faro told the banker, "I'd love to meet you someday across a poker table. You swallow a bluff like a hungry mud cat."

Chapter Three

Anthony Winchell was outside the main entrance to the St. Louis depot, sweating like a fat man on the Fourth of July. He paced back and forth, alternating anxious glances at his pocket watch with forlorn stares up and down the busy street.

From his vantage point in an alley across from the depot, Faro was deriving immense satisfaction from watching the banker's increasing anxiety. They were to have met at two in the afternoon, and it was twenty past two now. The train would be pulling out of the station in exactly five minutes.

If this business was on the up and up, Faro thought, then he was a gelding in a pasture full of fillies. Winchell had been exceptionally glib with the string of lies he told, but Faro had decades of experience in dealing with sharpies. The banker was a rank amateur compared to some of the con artists Faro had squared off against. At this point Faro still wasn't sure what the racket was, but he was convinced that he was supposed to be the monkey that got caught with the banana up his ass. It wasn't going to happen that way, though.

Faro had laid his plans carefully the night before. He had invested nearly an hour the previous evening thoroughly investigating the layout of first the depot, then the train yard outside. He knew which track his train was supposed to be on, and had already selected several routes of escape in case he needed to abort his plans. Before noon today he returned and left his luggage with a porter who promised to make sure it got on the proper train. By now his valise and case of gambler's "advantage" tools should already be in his compartment. Then he had scouted around the street outside until he found a good place from which to watch the depot entrance.

Gravedigger Smith and his two thugs arrived about one-thirty and went inside. Fifteen minutes later Winchell showed up and took his post at the front door. Now, assuming that the clerk was already on the train with the satchel, the entire cast was in place and it was up to Faro to raise the curtain.

Open relief showed on Winchell's face when he saw Faro emerge from the alley and start across the street toward the depot. "Damn you, Blake!" he stormed, drawing the attention of several passersby. "Where in the hell have you been?"

"Are you in the mood for explanations, or would you rather see me board that train before it pulls out?" Faro asked.

"Here," Winchell snapped, thrusting a train ticket and a long white envelope at Faro.

Faro accepted both, then opened the envelope and quickly counted the money inside. "There's only a thousand here," he said. It was what he figured would happen, but he still knew a protest was expected.

"You didn't expect me to pay you the whole amount at the start, did you?" the banker asked. "The rest of the money will be wired ahead to New Orleans, where my clerk will pick it up and pay you at the end of the trip."

"If it's not there, I'll be sending your man back to you a piece at a time," Faro warned. "And there's no telling what might become of the cargo he's carrying."

Winchell consulted his pocket watch for about the fifth time since they had been talking, then said, "You *must* hurry, Mr. Blake. The train is going to leave any minute now."

"I'll be on it," Faro assured him.

As he had hoped, Winchell did not accompany him to the boarding platform. No doubt he knew about the farewell party Faro had waiting for him and didn't want to be seen anywhere in the same vicinity. But Faro was better prepared this time for his encounter with Gravedigger Smith.

The long platform alongside the train was practically empty now. The other passengers were already on board, and the conductor was beginning to pick up the portable wooden steps at the end of every car. Down beside the tracks, a laborer with a five-gallon bucket of grease and a long brush was swabbing lubrication on the wheels of one of the passenger cars.

Smith and his two men spotted Faro as soon as he stepped out of the building and started for the train. He stopped and waited for them to come up to him. Smith took a stance directly in front of Faro, and the two bruisers flanked him on either side.

"You weren't planning to leave town without saying good-bye to your old sparring partners, were you, Blake?" the little man asked.

"To tell you the truth, I was looking forward to this meeting as much as you were, Smith," Faro replied. "I've got something for you."

"You better have something for me, tinhorn," Smith cautioned him.

Faro reached in the side pocket of his jacket and produced the envelope containing the thousand dollars. Smith snatched it out of his hand and eagerly began counting the bills inside. While he was doing that, Faro slipped his hand inside his coat to the loop he sometimes used to carry his sawed-off shotgun. Today the loop carried a different cargo. Faro's fingers fastened around the handle of the eighteen-inch oak club and he pulled it out in the open in one smooth motion.

Smith's men weren't prepared for trouble at that precise moment, especially since the debt had already been settled. Faro caught the man on his right with a solid blow to the side of his head. He toppled heavily off the platform into the dirt alongside the shiny steel rails. No more than a foot from where he lay, the train cars lurched as the distant locomotive pulled out the slack from between the cars.

Faro wasn't quite as successful with the man on his left. As he swung the club around, the man shifted his stance and the short oak stick glanced harmlessly off his shoulder. Faro caught a hard left jab to the jaw which staggered him back, but he used the club to ward off a roundhouse right which surely would have knocked him off his feet. The man roared in pain as the stick cracked across his knuckles, but it was going to take more than that to stop him. Faro knew what it would take. He straightened his right forearm in front of him and pulled his elbow tight against his side. His derringer slid comfortably out of his sleeve into his palm. It had taken a while for Faro to adapt his sleeve hold-out for use with the gun instead of with a playing card, but it had been worth the effort.

Gravedigger Smith had stayed close by during the fight, sure of the superiority of his man. Now he was amazed to find himself suddenly facing the business end of the vicious little weapon. He glanced nervously at Faro, then over toward the train, which was just beginning to jolt into motion. "What in the hell is this all about, Blake?" he asked. "Aren't you leaving on that train?"

"I am," Faro confirmed. "But I'm a vindictive bastard and before I go I want to savor the sweet taste of revenge." He pointed the derringer at Smith's henchman and said, "Why don't you be a nice gorilla and see if you can't find a banana somewhere. Go on. Get the hell out of here!" The man wandered off a few paces, then turned and gazed back in angry confusion. He cradled his injured hand in front of him like a treasure.

"All right, you little skunk," Faro told Smith. "Jump down off the platform."

"Goddamn, Blake!" Smith whined. "You ain't going to throw me under the train, are you? You know my brother-in-law is—"

"I know who your brother-in-law is, and if your sister's anything like you, I sure as hell pity him. *Now get down!*" By the time they had both hopped down to the level of the tracks, the train was beginning to pick up speed. It was going to be close.

Faro grabbed Smith by the scruff of the neck and bent him forward. "I would have liked to kick your ass man to man, Smith," he said hurriedly, "but I'm running out of time, and the fight would have been one man short anyway. So I guess I'll have to settle for this." He gave Smith's head a hard shove downward and plunged it in the bucket of thick axle grease which the workman had left sitting beside the track. Smith staggered off balance and for an instant it looked as if he might stumble beneath the wheels of the train. But then he caught himself, and when he began to straighten up, the bucket remained stuck on his head.

Faro's arm was nearly yanked out of its socket as he caught the railing of the last car, but he managed to get a foothold and swing himself up. The image of that dried-up little felon staggering blindly across the tracks with a grease bucket stuck on his head was a memory that Faro knew he would cherish for a long time.

Faro moved forward on the train through a few cars until he located his compartment. The interior was cramped but adequate. To his right was a long padded seat which extended out into a bed, and above, a second narrow bed could be folded out from the wall. In one corner was a tiny water closet, and beneath the window a small table could be folded up from the outside wall. To the left was a connecting door which led to the next compartment. As he expected, his valise and advantage tool case lay on the seat.

He took off his jacket, vest and shirt, then removed the sleeve hold-out, which was strapped across his back and down his right arm. After returning it to its proper place in the advantage tool case, Faro stepped into the water closet to wash up. As he was redressing, the conductor came around to punch his ticket.

"How long is it until the next stop?" Faro asked him.

"About twenty minutes," the man told him. "We have a half-hour layover in East St. Louis. From there we head south toward Cairo and then Memphis. If you're traveling on to New Orleans, you'll switch trains in Memphis at four tomorrow afternoon."

Faro's next duty, he decided, was to meet the person he had come on this trip to protect. He checked the load in his Reid's and slipped it in the pocket of his vest, then knocked on the door which supposedly connected his compartment with that of his charge. When he received no answer he waited a moment, then knocked again. Finally the door swung open.

The severe-looking woman who stood in the doorway had an unmistakable look of scorn on her face. Her brown hair was pulled straight back from her plain features in a schoolmarmish bun. She wore a drab brown traveling dress of unseasonably heavy wool which buttoned up to her throat in front and hung nearly to her ankles below. On first glance Faro took her to be a woman in her late middle years, but closer inspection revealed that she was younger. She was probably no more than twenty-five, but she seemed to be doing her damnedest to look twice that.

Faro disliked her instantly, and it was apparent that she shared the same feeling toward him.

"I think maybe there's been some mistake here," Faro stammered out. "I was looking for . . . well, I'm not exactly sure who, but I don't think it's you."

"Are you Mr. Faro Blake?" she asked. From the tone of her voice, she could be about to serve him a warrant.

"That's right," he answered. "And if you know my name, then you must be from the bank after all." Even as he spoke, his eyes settled on the satchel which he had seen the day before in Anthony Winchell's office. He hadn't figured on riding herd over a woman, and especially not one as drab and sour as this one.

"My name is Greta Wimbley, and I am the person you were hired to protect on this train," she told him. "I witnessed your disgraceful spectacle before we left the station and I want you to know I soundly disapprove." At any moment, he half expected her to haul out a wooden ruler and rap him across the knuckles with it for his sins. "The idea of this journey is *not* to call attention to ourselves," she continued, "but you seem to be the kind of man who has some trouble doing that."

"I was just wrapping up a little old business before I left the city," Faro told her. "You don't have to concern yourself with it."

"Mr. Blake, let's get something straight before we continue any further," she snapped. Her tone of voice grated on Faro's nerves like a nail on a slate chalkboard. "Until that satchel is delivered safely to its destination, everything you do or say is my concern. In the future I expect you to conduct yourself with more restraint and to keep constantly in mind your primary purpose in being here. Is that clear?"

Faro had to grit his teeth to keep from spilling out the profane reply which came immediately to mind. "I'll do my job, Miss Wimbley," he told her sourly. "That's not something you've got cause to worry about."

When Faro was alone again in his compartment, he took a seat by the window and began to watch the river sweeping past far below him. A shower was dappling the glass with raindrops, while off to the west the sun still shone brightly. For a few minutes he kept his eyes fixed on a thick rainbow which rose straight up from the center of the Mississippi. A small boat, bobbing on the churning surface of the river, passed straight through the base of the rainbow, and Faro found himself thinking that if the boat's occupants would just look down, they could probably spot the pot of gold. It was always someplace other than where you were.

A thud against the wall of the compartment next door brought his thoughts back to the present and to the abrasive young woman who was his traveling companion.

Faro didn't have much experience in dealing with women like Greta Wimbley, tediously proper spinsters whose ankles probably hadn't been sighted by mortal man since they had outgrown diapers. He had no real notion of what might motivate a woman of her kind, nor did he have any strong urges to find out. But surely for the sum of five hundred dollars a day, he could tolerate three days of swallowing any kind of bullshit she felt inclined to hand out.

Still, though, the encounter with Winchell's clerk had taken the luster off the good feelings he'd had over settling the score with Gravedigger and finally making his escape from St. Louis. He took a deck of cards from his advantage tool case and laid out two poker hands face up on the small table by the window, consoling himself with thoughts of how good it would feel three days from now to find himself in New Orleans with five hundred dollars cash in his wallet.

Chapter Four

Faro dined alone, enjoying the calm luxury of the railroad dining car. Often on the trains out West, a man knew he'd better stick a loaf of bread and a can of beans in his kit if he didn't want to starve on the long ride to wherever he was going. But here in the East, passengers received more elegant treatment during their travels.

The dining car was practically empty now. Greta had eaten first while Faro stayed behind to guard the satchel, then she had grudgingly consented to let him leave his compartment for a meal. The system seemed to be working out pretty well. They conducted most of their business past the briefly opened connecting door, and neither was subjected to the grating companionship of the other any longer than necessary. A couple of times Faro's curiosity got the best of him and he found himself with his eye to the keyhole of the door, wondering how a solemn wench like her passed her idle time. But just south of East St. Louis she either divined what he was doing or suspected him capable of such a thing, and she hung a blouse over the door knob, blocking his view.

Faro was halfway through his steak and his first bottle of Bordeaux when the door at the far end of the dining compartment opened and a young woman came in. *Now there's a woman!* Faro thought to himself. *I wonder why old Anthony Winchell doesn't have the good sense to keep that kind of courier around the good old Fidelity Trust?*

Cascades of shimmering blond hair surrounded a face that made a man's heart start thumping like a witch doctor with a new drum, and she had the kind of body that most men would kill to claim. Her silky yellow dress shimmered in the lamplight of the dining car, accenting the curves of her body with highlights and shadows. The neckline of the garment was scooped low in front, revealing a fine expanse of flawless breast, and as she passed by Faro her skirts rustled like an evening breeze in a pine forest. Beneath the soft veneer of innocence on her face was a subtle look of allure which lit a lustful flame in Faro.

She scarcely looked at him as she passed, but there was something about the vague smile on her lips which told him that she had seen enough to make her interested. He cursed the black waiter under his breath for seating her at a table to his rear.

The next time the waiter went by, Faro stopped him and asked that a bottle of the wine he was drinking be served to the young woman. After it was delivered, Faro turned in his seat and gave her a smile. Her eyes glistened as she raised her glass in a gesture of thanks before tasting its contents. After her first sip, her pink tongue darted out to retrieve a drop of the Bordeaux which lingered on the rim of the glass. Faro turned back to his plate and paid her no more attention until the steak was finished and his bottle of wine was empty. Then he signed his check, indicating Greta's compartment number, and rose from the table.

The lovely young woman's eyes fastened on him as soon as he turned. He thought he read a vague invitation in them, or at least a willingness to be approached. The rest of the diners had left by this time, and the waiter had discreetly dissolved into some cubbyhole at the opposite end of the car.

"The wine is delicious. Thank you," the young woman told him as he stopped beside her table. From the looks of things, she had hardly touched the broiled trout on her plate, but the wine bottle was half empty. Her eyes sparkled with the mellow beginnings of intoxication.

"I thought it was tasty," Faro agreed.

"Would you care to join me in finishing this bottle?" she offered. "I'm afraid if I drank the rest of it by myself, I might have trouble getting back to my compartment alone."

"I'll be glad to oblige," Faro grinned. He took a seat across the table from her and half filled the glass from the place setting there. After introducing himself, he learned in turn that her name was Charlotte Penrod and that she was on her way from Chicago to visit an ailing aunt in Memphis.

"I've been traveling for nearly two days now," Charlotte explained to him, "and I don't think I've ever been so bored in all my life. In one place I met an old lady from Peoria who asked me to sit and talk to her while she knitted some booties for her grand-daughter. After an hour with her, I thought, My God, there has to be something more interesting to do aboard a railroad train than this!" It was easy to see that the alcohol had loosened her tongue, and Faro was quick to order another bottle when hers was nearly gone. She gave Faro a sly look when the waiter uncorked it and refilled her glass, but she did not protest.

Over the second bottle of wine, the conversation eventually turned to Faro, and Charlotte was clearly impressed that she was sharing the company of a professional gambler who had traveled the Western frontier so extensively. Faro entertained her with a few of his best stories of fortunes gained and lost, as well as a sampling of savage Indian raids and bloody shoot-outs.

Almost as soon as he joined her, Faro started to realize where he and Charlotte would end up before the evening was over and what they would end up doing. The prospects made his blood race hotly in his veins, but he also realized that he must take care to insure that the union came about according to established procedures. An aura of seduction must prevail, and later if Charlotte found herself in need of an excuse as to why she permitted a perfect stranger on a train to take such liberties, she could explain to herself that he got her drunk and charmed her beyond her abilities to resist.

Midway through the second bottle of wine, Faro suggested that Charlotte might find some of the tools of his gambler's trade interesting. She quickly agreed that she would, and in a few minutes they found themselves weaving down the narrow passageway toward his compartment. When they arrived, he locked the connecting door to Greta's compartment, then the one leading out to the passageway. He couldn't hear any sounds coming from Greta's quarters, and he hoped she had already gone to bed.

Faro didn't light the lamp, but raised the window shades all the way up and let the soft moonlight bathe the compartment. The quarters were so cramped that there was hardly room for two people to move around at the same time, but under the circumstances that worked to their advantage. Charlotte let a slight lurch of the train throw her into Faro's arms, and once there, she was content to remain.

Faro enjoyed the look and feel of her for a moment before even trying to kiss her. The moonlight tinted the features of her lovely face a soft brown, and her half-opened eyes communicated an unmistakable message of sensuality. Her tongue ventured out to moisten her pale red lips, then her mouth remained slightly open. Her breasts were full and firm against his chest, and her thighs made soft thrilling contact against his. He let his hands journey lightly down from her waist to her hips as he leaned his head forward and touched their lips together. Charlotte closed her eyes and sighed submissively.

"I think I'm a little drunk," she admitted. She laid her head against his shoulder and held her body more firmly against him. "It feels marvelous."

Faro raised her chin with his hand and kissed her again, then let his lips stray down across her neck. The upper sleeves of her dress slid easily off her shoulders, and she seemed unaware when his fingers went to work on the buttons at the back of the dress. Her breathing was already beginning to quicken and a faint moan rose from her throat each time his lips and tongue located a sensitive area.

"Oh Faro, I shouldn't," she whispered. It was an obligatory protest.

Faro cupped her breasts in his palms and located her nipples with his thumbs through the light fabric of her clothing. They were firm and eager for release. "You shouldn't what?" he asked her.

"I don't know you at all," she explained. There was a breathless quality to her voice which showed that some inner power was already beginning to take control of her. "I shouldn't be letting any of this happen."

"Leave if you want to, Charlotte," he offered. "If you feel like you have to."

"I will," she vowed. He managed gently to slide the front of her dress and her undergarments down out of the way, and his hands enveloped the delicious bare flesh of her breasts. "In a minute I'll have to go back to my own compartment."

That was the last time the prospect of her leaving was mentioned, which hardly surprised Faro. What Charlotte Penrod lacked in sexual experience, she more than made up for with youthful enthusiasm and natural passion. Within a short time their clothing was cast aside and they lay in the middle of Faro's bed, naked and eager.

Without her clothing, Charlotte's body had a certain rare magnificence. In the moonlight her soft skin seemed almost translucent, but the flesh beneath was firm and healthy. His knowing caresses sent shivers of delight racing the length of her body, and when he enveloped first one nipple, then the other in his mouth, her back arched up and a lustful moan tumbled from her lips. He heightened the sensations for her by exploring down with his hand until his fingers grazed the lips of her moist feminine passageway and sought out the firm button of her clitoris.

When the young woman finally located the thick, hungry sapling which had sprouted between Faro's legs, her first touches were tentative. She lightly traced the length of it with her fingertips, then gripped it in her palm and gave it a soft squeeze. She raised up slightly to get a look at her newfound treasure. She gave him a shy, embarrassed smile and asked, "Does it bother you, me looking at it?"

"Hardly," Faro chuckled, rolling over on his back to give her better access to the object of her fascination.

"This probably sounds silly," Charlotte giggled, "but I've never really looked at one up close. They do get big, don't they?"

"I didn't take you for a virgin," Faro commented.

"Well, there's this boy in Chicago, and a couple of times . . ." she began hesitantly. "But it was never the same as this. We were always in a hurry, and there seemed to be so many clothes in the way. I mean, I knew he had one and all, but . . ." By then she had sat up beside him on the bed, and her hands were supplying him with so much pleasure that he hardly cared what she was saying. When her head tipped forward tentatively, Faro gave her a smile and an approving nod. She settled her lips over the end of his erect cock and drew it slowly into her mouth. With his hands on the back of her head, Faro gently and wordlessly instructed her in the most effective techniques of the oral act.

Minutes later when she finally came up for air, Faro caressed her cheek with his fingertips and suggested, "Why don't you try it on for size?"

"But shouldn't I be . . . ?" Charlotte asked. "Don't we have to rearrange ourselves or something?"

"Not necessarily," he grinned. He tugged at her leg, indicating that she should sit across him. When she was in position, he reached up to trace light circles around her nipples with his fingers as she slowly settled down on his erection. They traded smiles as they shared the initial moment of delight.

"It feels just like it belongs there!" Charlotte exclaimed in wonderment.

"I've got no complaints either," Faro told her. He pulled her body down on top of his, then arched his hips up and back, supplying them both with a renewed rush of pleasure.

As could be expected with a woman of her youth and vitality, Charlotte soon began to quicken the pace as her body sought the ultimate thrill to which it instinctively knew it was entitled. Faro put his experience to work to maintain a certain rhythm, though he soon found himself pinned to the bed by a bucking, frenzied female.

When her climax started, her moans began to rise from deep within her chest as her pelvis pounded without mercy against his. The fever pitch of Charlotte's excitement spurred Faro on to even greater efforts. Just when he finally sensed a decline in the young woman's racking orgasm, his cock throbbed almost unbearably and his hot juices surged into her.

Faro's first thought when the commotion started was that the train was about to be derailed. Then, as he gained control of his muddled thoughts, he realized that the source of the disturbance was a loud pounding on the wall of the next compartment. He sat up so suddenly that he tumbled Charlotte to the side and she fell off the edge of the bed. In an instant he was on his feet and rummaging through the tangled pile of clothing on the floor, searching for his jacket and his Reid's derringer.

The hammering had stopped by the time Faro unlocked the connecting door. He burst into Greta's compartment with the tiny gun ready, expecting to be confronted by immediate danger.

Greta Wimbley stood in the middle of her compartment, dressed in a cotton nightgown which shrouded her form from her shoulders to her toes. In her right hand she was holding a brown leather shoe, and after one look at her face, Faro knew that the only danger he might face would come from her. Her eyes scanned up and down his naked body, then settled on his face with a glare of unbridled fury.

"Mr. Blake! This is absolutely outrageous!" she yelled shrilly at him.

"Well goddamnit, I thought you were in some kind of danger," Faro stormed back at her. "I didn't have the time to put any clothes on."

"I'm not talking about that," Greta told him. "I'm talking about what you've been doing in there. I've never been exposed to anything so licentious and disgusting in all my life!"

"You wouldn't have been exposed to it, woman, if you hadn't started pounding on the wall with your shoe like a damn crazy woman," Faro snarled at her.

"But I could hear you in there! I could hear every disgusting whine and whimper, and finally I just couldn't tolerate it any longer. You have no right to haul your doxies in here for such scandalous activities when you're supposed to be protecting me."

"You can go to hell, too. As long as I do my job protecting you and that little satchel of papers over there, then anything else I decide to do is my own damn business."

Greta was quickly becoming unnerved, both by Faro's defiance and his nudity. Despite her anger, she just couldn't seem to keep her eyes from roving down his body. At last she turned away from him completely.

"Don't think I won't report this incident to my employer, Mr. Winchell," she warned. "He's going to be made aware of every disgusting detail, and I can assure you that he will not be pleased."

"I don't care what you report to who, just so long as you come up with that five hundred dollars when I deliver you to New Orleans," Faro replied as he turned away.

By the time he returned to his compartment and closed the connecting door, Charlotte Penrod was nearly dressed. "Shitfire!" Faro muttered disgustedly to himself. Her back was turned to him as she buttoned her dress, and her shoulders were shaking, either with anger, humiliation or both. He realized how useless it would be at this point to try either to console her or convince her to stay with him.

When she finished dressing, the young woman wiped her eyes with her fingertips and turned to Faro. She had a look of betrayal on her face and she seemed to be fighting to hold back the tears. "I hurt my elbow when you threw me on the floor," she said, pouting.

"I'm sorry," he told her. "And I'm sorry the evening had to end this way, too."

"Well, it wasn't all bad," she said, finally offering him a shy, teary smile. "I guess if I set my mind to it, I could just remember the good parts."

"Why don't you try that?" Faro said. He gave her a soft kiss and a light pat on the rear end just before she slipped out into the passageway.

Chapter Five

Faro lay awake in bed for a long time that night. He was still keyed up from the angry encounter with Greta, and he had yet to purge his mind of a few remaining regrets concerning Charlotte Penrod. The scent of her perfume lingered on the bedcovers, reminding him of the continuing pleasure they might have shared under different circumstances.

Dealing with Winchell's staid female clerk was proving to be more of a trial that Faro had anticipated, and he kept returning to thoughts of simply abandoning her. After the incident tonight, who could blame him if he gathered up his baggage and left the train at one of the numerous small towns along the way? He could be gone before she even realized it. But that would mean giving up the final five hundred dollars of his payment, and what would he do with himself in some one-horse whistlestop without any money and no readily available way to earn any?

It would be better, he decided, to go on at least as far as Memphis. The last he had heard, Nell Garvin, an old friend and sometime lover, was now living in Memphis. She might be able to steer him toward some gambling action in her area. He thought surely he could tolerate being in the vicinity of Greta Wimbley for the few more hours it would take to reach that city.

Finally the rhythmic clatter of the train's wheels on the steel rails lulled him into an uneasy slumber. He dreamed of making love to a sobbing, petulant Charlotte while Greta pounded him furiously across his backside with a shoe. Every time he tried to turn and make Greta leave him alone, Charlotte bawled even louder and he was forced to redouble his efforts to placate her. He awoke with a dull stone ache below his bladder.

Faro tried to ignore the first couple of dull thumps he heard coming from Greta's compartment. He figured she was probably burning the midnight oil, compiling her scathing report to Winchell, and had flown into a fresh rage over her trampled sensibilities. But his curiosity was aroused when he glanced toward the door and saw that no band of light shined beneath it. Whatever Greta was doing, she was doing it in the dark. He retrieved his Reid's from the table by the window and moved to the door.

"Hey!" he called out. "Are you okay in there?" He pulled on his trousers as he listened for a response.

When Greta didn't reply, Faro tried the latch. It was locked on her side. "You'd better answer up, woman, or I'm coming through!" he called out to her. With his ear to the door, he heard another dull thump and a noise which could have been a stifled cry.

Faro drew away from the door, then slammed his shoulder against it, destroying the latch which held it closed. As the door flew open, he sensed something coming at him in the darkness. He ducked his head to avoid the full impact of the pistol barrel, but he caught a glancing blow across the back of his skull. Stunned, he glimpsed a dark form rushing out of the compartment.

"Greta? Where are you?" he called out in alarm. He heard a moan from the bed and stumbled over to where she lay. A trickle of fresh blood glistened below a cut at the edge of her hairline, and her eyes looked dreamy, unable to focus. "Are you okay?" Faro asked.

"He's got it! He took it!" Greta mumbled faintly. "You've got to stop him."

"But what about you?" Faro asked.

"You've got to get that satchel back!" Greta insisted. Her tone of voice showed that she wasn't seriously hurt.

"Okay, but I'll be back as fast as I can," he promised. "Don't leave this compartment."

Faro reached the passageway outside in time to see a man disappear through the door which led to the next car behind. He leaped forward with his derringer ready and took up the chase. When he reached the open walkway between the two cars, the train lurched and he almost lost his balance in the darkness, but he grabbed hold of the handle of the door in front of him and caught himself.

The next car was an ordinary passenger car filled with sleeping travelers slumped over in their seats. Faro stopped just inside the door and stared down the dark, empty aisle ahead. The man hadn't had time to get to the far end of the aisle and out the other door, so Faro knew he must still be somewhere in this car. Cautiously he started forward, gazing down at every sleeper he passed and trying to catch a glimpse of the stolen satchel.

Near the opposite end of the car, a faint noise behind him alerted him to danger. As he turned, the pistol barrel caught him on the side of his head and tumbled him sideways into the lap of an enormous female passenger. His attacker leaped for the nearby door and Faro raised the Reid's hoping for a clear shot. But the startled fat woman began pounding him with her meaty fists as she cut loose with a series of shrill screams. His shot flew wild, shattering the glass in the door above his opponent's head. Faro clipped the woman in the jaw with his elbow, and managed to scramble out of her clutches.

By then most of the passengers in the car were awake and a few of them were on their feet. Faro shoved his way to the door and rushed out. The next car he came to was a baggage car, and the door at this end of it was locked. That left his opponent with only two alternatives, up or out, and the moonlit landscape was rushing by the train at an alarming speed. Faro took hold of the ladder mounted on the end of the baggage car and began to climb.

He caught sight of the pair of legs just as his head cleared the top of the car. He dodged a kick aimed at his head, then caught the leg with his hand and gave it a sharp twist. When the man went down atop the baggage car, his pistol went clattering out of his hand and over the edge, but he managed to hold onto the satchel. As Faro scrambled up the ladder, his opponent leaped to his feet and started away again. Faro raised the Reid's and took aim, then hesitated. If he shot now, both the stranger and the satchel he was carrying might topple over the edge before he could do anything about it. That would mean no money in New Orleans if he went that far, and no answers about who this character was and why he was so interested in a bag full of bank records.

He rose to his feet and continued the chase, knowing there wasn't much train left. At the end of the line, the stranger would be forced either to surrender his cargo and start talking or take a long hard fall off the back of the train.

The next car they scampered across was another baggage car, and following that was the caboose. As Faro climbed down to the landing at the front of the caboose, the man stepped out of the shadows and tried one more time to shove him off the train. Faro pointed the Reid's at his head and convinced him it was a bad idea.

"All right, friend, if we're real careful from here on," Faro told the stranger, "then maybe we can handle this business without anybody getting hurt. First off, I want you to set that satchel down and step away from it."

The man hesitated. His eyes strayed to the side and he seemed to be considering taking the jump.

"If you try it, you'll be dead before your feet hit the ground," Faro cautioned him. "Put it down and back off." Finally the man complied with the instructions. "Now let's go in there and talk awhile," Faro said.

A single kerosene lamp burned in the empty caboose. Faro motioned with the Reid's toward a bench along one wall and said, "Sit if you want to." The man tossed a scowl at Faro and parked his short, husky frame on the bench. He wore a drab brown suit with a cheap white shirt and tie, and by the slight bulge under his left arm, Faro knew that the pistol he had lost probably belonged in the holster there. His menacing face was pocked with ancient acne scars, and he had a certain shrewd look in his eye which kept Faro on his guard.

"You know, the only reason I'm in the state of mind to treat you halfway decent," Faro explained, "is that you had three chances back there to nail me with your pistol and you never did use it. What kind of robber are you, anyway?"

"I'm not a thief," the man growled.

"Then tell me who in the hell you are."

"Get fucked," the man said.

Faro backhanded him across the jaw with his knuckles, half knocking him off the bench, then brought the Reid's to bear again before the stranger could do anything about it.

"Don't start being a son of a bitch on me," Faro said.

"You're in big trouble, fella," the stranger warned, "you and that woman back there. Sure, I'll tell you who I am. It can't hurt anything. My name's Turk Bishop and I'm a private detective. I've been hired by the Fidelity Trust Bank in St. Louis to recover that satchel."

"What in the hell are you talking about?" Faro exclaimed. "Are you going to tell me that Winchell sent *you* after *us?*"

"I was hired by the president of the bank, Mr. Peter Sylvester," Bishop explained. "He told me that some spinster clerk in his bank had made off with some important documents, and that she might not be traveling alone."

"That sounds like a crock of shit to me," Faro scoffed. But he really wasn't so sure. He had been suspicious of this business from the start, and now for some reason he found himself more inclined to believe this man's story than the one Winchell told him.

"If you were smart, you could still come out of this business in pretty good shape," Bishop told him. "They want that satchel back, but they don't want any to-do about it because of their stockholders. That's why they hired me instead of taking the matter to the police. So if you just handed it over and backed off, I could take it on back to St. Louis and you'd be in the clear. I've got credentials in my pocket proving who I am." Very carefully the man produced a leather wallet from the breast pocket of his coat. The card inside which identified him as a private detective looked authentic enough, but Faro still wasn't convinced.

"I think it's time I found out what's so goddamn important about what's inside this thing," Faro decided.

The clasp of the satchel had a small lock on it, but it was easily jimmied with a pen knife. Then Faro unfastened the clasp and opened the satchel. Neither he nor the detective was prepared for what they saw inside.

"Godawmightydamn!" Bishop muttered. "I never seen that much money in all my life!"

Faro took one bundle of twenty-dollar bills out and examined it in amazement, then dropped it back in with the rest. The satchel was stuffed with fat bundles of currency.

"Did you know this thing was full of money?" Faro asked the detective.

"Hell no! They told me it was only bank records and suchlike. How much you figure is in there?"

"Fifty, maybe sixty thousand. At least."

Bishop was mesmerized by the money. He

couldn't tear his gaze away from the satchel, and Faro recognized a particular gleam in his eye which he had seen many times before. It was the look of unbridled greed.

"Split two ways, that's still one hell of a lot of money," the detective suggested.

"And not split at all, it's even more," Faro replied. He was even more careful to keep the derringer trained on his prisoner now. This much wealth could inspire a man to take desperate chances.

Faro realized that he faced some hard choices now. Even he wasn't above having his head turned by this much money, but he still wasn't completely sure whose money it was and what he would become involved in if he simply took it. But one thing of which he was sure was that this man with him posed a definite threat, not only to the money, but probably to Faro's life as well.

Just then the door at the front of the caboose swung open and an angry male voice demanded, "What in the hell is going on there?"

Instinctively Faro turned his head to see who had come in, and the detective chose that instant to make his move. He kicked the hand which held the Reid's, knocking the weapon from Faro's grip, then lashed out with his fist. Bishop's short, powerful arms propelled his knuckles like a pile driver into Faro's jaw, sprawling him back across the caboose. Then the detective snatched up the satchel and made a leap for the rear door. Apparently he had decided that this much money was worth some cuts and bruises, and perhaps a couple of broken bones. He was going to jump!

Faro rolled toward the door and caught Bishop's leg just as he was going out. Bishop swung the satchel around and hit Faro with it, but Faro held on and managed to get a hand on the detective's other leg. In a moment they both lay in a pile in the open doorway, scrambling for possession of the satchel as they attempted to punch, gouge, bite or otherwise disable one another. The startled conductor had stopped a few paces away, either too cautious or too confused to enter the fight.

As the two combatants rolled out onto the landing at the back of the caboose, Bishop managed to get to his feet. Both he and Faro had a grip on the handles of the satchel, and neither had any intention of letting go. As the detective raised one foot to stomp Faro, Faro lashed out with his own foot and caught his opponent between the legs. Bishop roared in pain and let go of the satchel. He staggered back, barely catching himself with a handhold on the railing before falling off the train. He looked like his balls were lodged somewhere in his throat.

Faro pitched the satchel out of the way and rose to his feet. "I think it's about time I punched your ticket, Bishop," he said. He kicked the detective hard in the midsection. Bishop's quick yelp of surprise was cut short as his body struck the ground beside the tracks and rolled out of sight down an embankment.

By the time Faro reentered the caboose, the conductor had gathered his wits enough to pick up the derringer. He stood pointing it at Faro, and he looked disturbed enough to pull the trigger.

"I know I should have turned him over to you instead of throwing him off," Faro said, "but I was just too pissed off. What kind of maniacs do you let on your train anyway?"

"Huh?" the startled conductor asked. He wasn't prepared for Faro's sudden anger.

"Don't you have any kind of security at all?" Faro demanded.

"What are you talking about?"

"I'm talking about *rape!*" Faro stormed at him. "That son of a bitch damn near raped my fiancé, and when I broke in on him, he stole this bag from her and took off. I swear, I'm going to raise some hell with the president of the line about this!"

"Now, before you go off half cocked . . ." the conductor stammered.

"Give me my gun!" Faro demanded. He reached out, and the confused conductor permitted him to retrieve the Reid's. With a feeling of relief, Faro stashed it in his trousers pocket.

"It might be better to keep this whole thing quiet," the conductor suggested. "Consider the young lady."

"But goddamn . . . !"

"Think of her reputation," the conductor went on. "The man's gone, and if you raise a stink, it will only embarrass her more."

"Maybe you're right," Faro said, calming at last. "I've got to go see how she is, and I'll think about what you said. It might be better if all of us just let the whole thing drop."

When Faro got back to her compartment, Greta was sitting on the edge of her bed, examining the wound on her forehead with a small hand mirror. She had cleaned herself up and the flow of blood had slowed to a mere trickle, but she was going to have a fine lump there in the morning. From the throbbing in his battered head, Faro knew that for the next few days, he too would be carrying around some reminders of this night.

"Did you get it?" she asked, leaping to her feet.

When she saw the satchel in Faro's hands, she exclaimed "Thank goodness!" and made a grab for it. Faro stopped her with a hand in the middle of her chest and shoved her back onto the bed. For a moment, Greta was too startled to get back up.

"I've got it all right, but I'm not so sure I'm ready to turn it back over to you," he told her angrily. "Back there in the caboose, I took a look inside. I decided I wanted to know exactly what I was putting my ass on the line for."

"You had no right!" Greta yelled. "It doesn't belong to you!"

"But the big question is," Faro told her, "who does it belong to?" His nerves were still taut from the fight with Bishop, and he was in no mood to respond to her attempts at intimidation. Right now he felt more like wringing her neck than taking any of her crap.

"The money's being transferred to one of Fidelity Trust's affiliates in London for a major investment," Greta began. "We had to keep the transfer secret because of the nature of the business, but I can assure you that—"

"Nope. Try again."

"All right," she admitted. "If you must know, it's mine, mine and Anthony's. For years we've been investing our earnings wisely, and now finally we've decided we have enough accumulated to—"

"Damn you, woman!" Faro lashed out. He tossed the satchel aside, then picked Greta up by the lapels of her robe and shook her. "Can't you see that you're dealing with a dangerous man here? If you keep trying to spoon-feed me this line of crap, I won't be responsible. I want to hear the truth, and I want it quick!"

Greta's eyes grew large with fear as it began to soak in that she could be in as much danger now from her bodyguard as she had been earlier from her attacker. "Please . . ." she muttered meekly as the tears began to gather in her eyes.

"Are you going to start bawling on me, for Christ's sake?" Faro growled with disgust. He let go of her clothing and she fell back limply on the bed.

"I can't help it," Greta sobbed. "All of this has been so frightening to me." Now that the waterworks were turned on, Faro realized that he might as well let it run its cycle before he tried to get any more information from her. Any further attempts to interrogate her were only going to increase the problem.

Greta sniffed and sobbed for a while, dabbing at her eyes and nose with a corner of her robe and throwing him those baleful glances which never failed to make a man feel guilty no matter who was in the right. When she finally began to calm, Faro said, "Now will you please tell me what the hell is going on here? I promise I won't hurt you, but I will leave if you don't shed some light on this business pretty soon. And if I go, that goes with me," he added, pointing to the money.

"We stole it," Greta admitted. From the look in her puffy, red eyes, Faro believed that they might be getting to the heart of the matter at last. "Anthony and I stole it from the bank."

That was the conclusion Faro had already come to, though she and Winchell hardly seemed likely accomplices for such a crime.

"Anthony had the whole thing planned before he even talked to me about it," Greta continued. "I was never sure it was a good idea, but he said we could use the hundred thousand dollars to go away together."

"There's one hundred thousand dollars in that bag?" Faro exclaimed.

"Give or take a few thousand. Anthony is supposed to meet me in New Orleans later, and after we're married, we'll probably catch a boat for England or France. We'll have the money to go anywhere and do anything we want."

"Well after what happened tonight," Faro told her, "we're going to have to assume that something's gone haywire with your plan. Go back to the start and tell me every detail of how the two of you pulled it off."

Greta explained that a day and a half ago, she and Winchell had remained at work late after the bank closed on Friday afternoon. When everyone else was gone, they had simply opened the vault and stuffed the satchel with all the bundles of large denomination bills they could find. The bank would be closed all weekend, and by the time the theft was discovered on Monday, Greta would be almost all the way to New Orleans.

"Anthony's story was going to be that he had gone home shortly after everyone else, leaving me in charge of locking up," Greta said. "Such a thing was not uncommon. He would also spread the story that I had been acting strange lately, and that he had seen me a couple of times in public in the company of a rather seedy looking character, a fancy dresser and a real charmer, but obviously unscrupulous nonetheless."

"Meaning me, I suppose," Faro grumbled.

"Precisely, Mr. Blake. The obvious implication would be that I had fallen victim to this man's seductions, and that he had convinced me to steal the money so we could go away together. Eventually when the money was not recovered, Anthony planned to accept responsibility for letting the robbery take place and resign his job in disgrace. Later he would join me in New Orleans."

"This fellow Winchell sounds like a real gallant boyfriend, Greta," Faro observed. "He planned the whole thing so that the blame would fall on you and me, but in the end he still gets his cut of the loot. Or maybe he plans to eventually end up with all of it."

"No, that's not the way it is at all!" Greta protested. "We're going to get married and travel the world together. We're going to do all the things that neither of us ever had the chance to do before, and someday we're going to settle down in another city and start a new life together. We've discussed it all, and we've agreed how it's going to be."

Gazing down at the plain young woman who sat on the bed before him, Faro could easily understand how Winchell could ram such a dream down her throat and talk her into believing that it would come true. Greta Wimbley had probably spent most of her adult life as a drab spinster, a total stranger to romance and excitement of any kind. He could see her accepting the scheme like a bass swallowing a hook, but it was harder to envision Winchell following through with his part of the bargain. For the moment, though, Faro decided not to destroy her illusions.

"Here's our problem now, Greta," Faro told her. "The man I threw off the back of this train said he was a private detective hired by Peter Sylvester, the president of Fidelity Trust, to recover that satchel. That means they already know about the robbery.

And since Turk Bishop was on this train, they must have known about it before we left St. Louis. How do you think that happened?"

"I don't know," Greta exclaimed. "Any number of things could have gone wrong, I suppose. Maybe Mr. Sylvester went to the bank early Saturday morning and discovered the money was missing. And because of that, Anthony might have been compelled to tell his story before he intended to. I just don't know, Faro. Honestly, I don't know what went wrong."

"I believe you, but it changes our situation considerably. Winchell hired me to escort a clerk and some bank records to New Orleans, not a satchel full of stolen money and the woman who stole it. I'll be damned if I'll take the rap for an asshole like him."

"You have to help me, Faro," Greta pleaded. "I don't know what to do, and I'm so afraid!"

"The only thing I *have* to do is cover my own ass," Faro told her. "And right now the best way to do that seems to be to take the money back."

"You can't do that! Don't you see? You're already implicated."

"But if I gave it all back to them and explained the situation . . ."

"Then it would be your word against that of the vice president of the bank," Greta reminded him. "You're a gambler without a cent to your name, and Anthony Winchell has been with the Fidelity Trust Bank for fourteen years. Who do you think the police would believe?"

Considered in that light, Faro realized what a mess he might be stepping into if he went back to St. Louis. He had paid enough short-term visits to the insides of jail cells to realize that they weren't the sort of places he would like to live in on a permanent basis.

"Even now they won't know your name, Faro," Greta continued. "Anthony was just going to say that I went off with some man. When you deliver me to New Orleans, you can collect the rest of your money and nothing will be hanging over your head. It could still work out."

"Yeah, or it could blow up in our faces like a keg of blasting powder," Faro pointed out. "What that private detective almost got away with proves that. If I did decide to go on south with you, we'd have to renegotiate the terms of our agreement."

"What do you mean?"

"I mean the stakes are a hell of a lot higher now, and the payment for my services will have to go up too."

"I'll double the amount you have coming," Greta offered.

"I was thinking more in terms of taking that five hundred and adding another zero to it," he said. "Under the circumstances, we both know that I could demand a lot more than that and get it."

The five-thousand-dollar figure was difficult for Greta to swallow, but eventually she nodded her head in agreement. There was little else she could do, and she seemed to understand that he could take it all, right then and there, if he chose.

"And another thing," Faro went on. "From this moment, I'm in complete charge. If you expect to reach New Orleans in one piece and with your little nest egg intact, you're going to have to let me handle things in my own way. Agreed?"

Greta nodded again.

"All right, you'll be spending the rest of the night with me, and when mealtime comes, you can go out and bring something back to the compartment while I guard the money. We should reach Memphis in another few hours, and I've got a friend there who might be willing to lend us a hand."

Chapter Six

The driver stopped his buggy in front of a large, two-story house on a tree-lined suburban street and turned to his passengers. "This is it," he announced to Faro and Greta.

Looking up at the house, Faro thought it was fine enough to be the home of the mayor of Memphis rather than the residence of his old friend, Nell Garvin. The walls and trim of the building had recently received a fresh coat of paint, and the grounds were immaculately manicured. Low hedges lined the brick walk which led to the front door, and a neat white gazebo in the side yard was surrounded by a lovely flower garden. The yard was well shaded by towering oaks and maples, and a driveway around the side led to a long white stable in back. Nell must be doing all right for herself these days.

When the buggy was gone, Faro and Greta paused on the sidewalk out front amidst their luggage.

"What I don't understand is how that driver came straight to this house without your even giving him a street address," Greta said. "Your friend must be well known here in Memphis."

"Wherever Nell goes, she has a way of getting known around town fairly quickly," Faro told her.

Up until now, Faro had revealed very little to Greta about his friend Nell Garvin. Considering Greta's prudish nature, he guessed that she might rebel if she knew beforehand the type of place that they would be visiting. Once inside, she would understand everything soon enough. In a moment they started toward the house.

Greta had been surprised when he told her that they would be leaving the train in Memphis rather than continuing to New Orleans. Faro had assured her that he knew what he was doing and reminded her of the terms of their agreement. She had to trust him.

As they left the train station and loaded their luggage into a horse-drawn cab, Faro had watched closely to see if anyone seemed to be following them or observing them, but he saw no one. It was possible, he decided, that Bishop had been the only one on their trail, and with him out of the way, they might be in the clear for a while. But, with the amount of money at stake, he did not delude himself into thinking that they were completely safe.

The ride across town to the quiet street where Nell lived had been a pleasant one. Memphis was a lovely city at this time of year, and their trip had taken them through one of its nicest parts. They were lucky, Faro realized, not to have reached Memphis during one of the dreaded yellow fever epidemics which periodically ravaged her population.

A black maid greeted them at the front door of the

house. She was pretty with chocolate skin that shone with vitality. The unusual uniform she wore made Greta stare in amazement. Her neatly starched, blue and white cotton dress stopped a few scant inches down her thighs, and she wore the front unbuttoned nearly to her navel. A good portion of her bare chest was in view, and her nipples pushed noticeably against the light fabric.

"We're here to see Miss Garvin," Faro told the girl. "Is she in?"

"Yessir, she's here," the maid said, giving him a bright smile. "You can wait in the parlor if you like."

Once they were in the parlor, Faro settled himself on a high-backed, brocade love seat and watched the young maid flounce out of the room.

"Did you see how that young woman was dressed?" Greta hissed indignantly.

"I tend to notice that sort of thing." Faro grinned.

"My word! Who would hire such a brazen creature for a household servant? She's bound to stir the baser instincts in every man who sees her."

"That seems likely," he chuckled.

Faro had to bite his tongue to keep from laughing out loud when a door across the room opened a minute later and another woman entered the room. She carried a sandwich in one hand and a glass of milk in the other, and when Greta fixed her eyes on her, the bank clerk's jaw dropped open as if it was weighted. The new arrival wore only a scanty pair of silk panties and a pair of white net stockings supported by a garter belt. Her breasts were enormous, bobbing from side to side as she walked. Her form was plump and her face was round and wholesomely pretty.

"Oh, hello!" she greeted them brightly. "I didn't know we were open yet. I guess I'd better go get dressed." She started across the room, then paused and looked back at Greta. "Are you going to join us here, honey?" she asked.

"I . . . I don't think . . ." Greta stammered. She was too dumbfounded to put a coherent sentence together.

"Well if you are, don't worry about the way you look now. Me and the girls will fix you up just fine," the woman promised.

When she was gone, Greta turned to Faro and demanded, "What sort of place have you brought me to? Good heavens! Are we in what I think we're in?"

"My dear Miss Wimbley"—Faro smiled at her— "you are now sitting in the parlor of one of the classiest brothels in Memphis, run by the shrewdest whore this side of the French Quarter. I would have told you sooner, but I figured you wouldn't take too well to the idea of coming here."

"You are absolutely correct, sir," Greta told him. "I resent your bringing me here and I demand to be taken away immediately."

"Go if you want to, lady," Faro replied calmly. "But leave that." He pointed to the satchel which sat on the floor at her feet. "Either we do things my way, as you agreed, or the game's over."

"But Faro!" Greta pleaded. "This is outrageous. No decent woman would be caught dead in a place like this!"

"Not too many decent women go around robbing banks, either," Faro pointed out to her, "so don't start getting all righteous on me. The fact is, you care about that money more than you care about your so-called decency, so while we're here, you'll just shut up and do what you're told. Have you got that straight?"

Anger flared in Greta's eyes, but she reluctantly nodded her head in agreement. As long as he had the hundred thousand dollars to use as a weapon against her, he knew that she would continue to do exactly as he instructed her.

Soon a woman appeared in the doorway to the right. She was dressed in a flowing gown of yellow satin which perfectly complemented her pale blond hair. Her hair was arranged in an elaborate style on top of her head, with curling ringlets hanging down along both sides of her face. Diamond earrings sparkled on her ears, and the diamond necklace around her neck followed the contours of her low-cut neckline. Beneath the demure smile on her face was a look of intelligence and subtle cunning. She swept the room with her eyes, seeming to take in every detail at a glance. Then her gaze fell on Faro and her smile widened.

"It's good to see you, Faro," she said in a voice fairly oozing with dignity and composure. "Have you brought me a proselyte?"

Greta was aghast at the suggestion, but wisely chose to remain silent.

"Hello, Nell," Faro said warmly, rising from his seat and going to her. She accepted his kiss with a certain measure of reserve. "Actually, I was traveling through Memphis with this lady and I heard you were in business here now. I just wanted to stop by and see how you are."

"I'll accept that for the time being," Nell told him. "Now please introduce me to your friend."

The women greeted one another with all the cordiality of two starving wolves meeting over the carcass of a dead rabbit. They surveyed each other with like amounts of cool disdain, and for a moment Faro thought the fur might soon begin to fly simply because of the looks they were exchanging. He was quick to intercede.

"How long has it been, Nell?" Faro asked. "If I remember right, the last time we were together was out in California when you were having so much trouble with that bruiser. What was his name?"

"Beaumont Bosworth," Nell reminded him. "That was almost two years ago, and it was a time in my life that I would love to forget."

"It was a nasty piece of business with that murderer, but you and I got to call the turn in the end, didn't we? And there were a few good times mixed in there too."

For an instant, a look of genuine affection registered on Nell's face as she recalled what he was talking about. The probing glance which she gave him bore a host of messages.

"My life has settled down considerably since then," Nell continued at last. "Soon after that, I came back here and bought out Madame Larue when she decided to retire from the business. Every one of my girls is top quality merchandise, and you wouldn't believe how much these city fellows can be persuaded to pay for their pleasures."

"I'm glad you're doing so well," Faro said. A quick glance at Greta showed how little she was interested in Nell's shoptalk. "Listen, Nell. We've been traveling for two days straight now. Have you got someplace where Miss Wimbley could freshen up and maybe take a rest?"

"Yes, of course," Nell replied. She seemed pleased by the prospects of parting company with the somber young clerk, and Faro admitted to himself that the idea appealed to him, too. There were a couple of reasons why he wanted to be alone with Nell for a while. One was to explain to her the real reasons why he was here, and the other flashed through his mind each time his eyes began to wander down the front of her dress.

Greta went along reluctantly as the black maid escorted her to an upstairs room recently vacated by one of Nell's ex-employees, but she was clearly displeased. Faro didn't let it worry him. The main thing was to have her out of his way for a few hours.

As soon as they were alone, Nell began to shed some of her unnecessary reserve. She was one of those remarkable women who could change personality and temperament faster than most women could change a dress. In the wink of an eye, she could transform herself from a cool, aloof lady to a saucy, seductive tramp. Faro had been watching her doing it for years, and he still wasn't sure who the real Nell Garvin was. In fact, she was probably both personalities.

Nell went to a sideboard and poured them both a healthy slug of whiskey. "What rock did you have to turn over to come up with *that* one?" Nell asked him. "Don't tell me the great Faro Blake has fallen so low that he's taken to servicing matrons and spinsters for his daily bread."

"Not hardly," Faro chuckled. "After the last couple of days with Greta Wimbley, I'm not sure I could do her any good even if she did want to pay me for it. I've just been hired to escort her from St. Louis to New Orleans. She's carrying some important papers for the bank she works for." He had decided earlier that it wouldn't be necessary to tell Nell everything about his and Greta's situation. One of the intriguing sides of his long-time relationship with Nell Garvin was that they both knew they could never trust the other completely. That's what kept them on their toes when they ended up together.

"Well, it sure was thoughtful of you to stop off here just to see me," Nell said. She was baiting him. "Now that I'm doing so well, it seems like every time I see an old friend, they always end up wanting something from me."

Faro set his glass down and rested his hands on Nell's sides, pulling her gently to him. "What I want from you is the same thing I wanted the first time I set eyes on you all those years ago," he said.

No matter how long they had been separated, a thrilling energy always passed between Faro Blake and Nell Garvin as soon as they were reunited. Faro had quit trying to understand it. All he knew for sure was that the touch of her body against his could make the hair on the back of his neck stand on end and fill him with the overwhelming horniness of a randy youngster on his first visit to the town tramp.

"It's good to see you haven't changed," Nell purred, settling into his arms like a kitten in a sewing basket. Her kiss contained all the lust and intensity that he remembered so well, and she was as eager to get to their first item of business as he was.

"Come on, let's go through here," she said, leading him to a doorway at the back of the parlor. "We're supposed to open for business soon, but the girls can handle things for the first hour or two."

Faro grinned. "Or three or four."

"Don't promise a girl something that you can't deliver, Mr. Blake," Nell teased.

"We'll see."

Nell's personal quarters consisted of a two-room suite on the ground floor of the house. The first room was a combination sitting room and office. A large oak desk sat by a window overlooking the garden behind the house. Across the room was a long, overstuffed couch and a couple of easy chairs with small oak tables beside them. Through a partially opened door at the far end of the room Faro glimpsed part of a large, canopy bed with scarlet accessories.

A bottle of wine in a bucket of ice sat on the corner of Nell's desk. Noticing it, Faro asked, "Were you expecting company?"

"I spotted you when you were coming up the walk with your lady friend," Nell admitted. "I had my maid, Tessie, bring this back here while I was out front with the two of you."

She picked up the wine and started for the bedroom, but when Faro tried to follow, she halted him at the door with a hand on his chest. "Give me a couple of minutes to get things ready," Nell told him. "It's been a long time for us and I want everything to be just right. I'll let you know when to come in." Faro grinned with amusement as she closed the door between them.

Though she believed she was keeping her long-term designs on him secret, Faro had been aware for years that deep in her heart Nell Garvin cherished the hope that someday the two of them would become something more than occasional lovers whenever they happened across one another during their travels. Faro had never considered himself a settling down kind of man, and he had never encouraged her to think in those terms. But still he had to admit to himself that if that day ever came for him, he could sure do a lot worse than to tie up with Miss Nell Garvin.

A few minutes later, he heard a soft summons from the adjoining room. He went to the door and opened it, then paused in the doorway to survey the scene of seduction which Nell had prepared for him.

She was reclined in the middle of the huge bed,

wearing a long silken gown which covered her like a pale morning fog. The details of her body were faintly visible beneath the wispy yellow material, creating an effect somehow more seductive than if she had worn nothing at all. The bottle of wine was open, and two half-filled glasses sat on a table beside the bed. The French doors along the back wall were open and the light curtains there stirred in a warm afternoon breeze blowing in from the garden. The room was bathed in pale yellow sunlight.

"Looks like you've gone all classy on me, Nell honey," Faro commented with a smile of appreciation for her efforts. "You've come a long ways from the backwoods of Arkansas, haven't you?"

"There's still plenty of that hot-tailed little Arkansas tramp left in me, as you've found out often enough," Nell said. "But I thought it might be fun this way."

"I've sure got no objections," he said.

When he went over and sat down on the edge of the bed beside her, Nell picked up one of the glasses and held it to his lips so he could drink. Then she set the glass aside and started massaging the tense muscles at the back of his neck. As the massage continued, Nell deftly removed his clothes a piece at a time. Soon he found himself stretched out naked on the bed with a pair of skilled hands kneading and relaxing every portion of his body from head to foot. She rubbed some sort of oil into his skin which smelled like sweet fresh herbs, bringing every inch of his skin alive with delightful sensations.

When at last he lay on his back before her and her attentions began to move down his chest toward his midsection, Faro knew the real fun was about to start. She oiled down her hands and brought him instantly to erection with her soft, slick caresses.

Faro laid his head back and closed his eyes, feeling a rare sense of contentment envelop him. At the moment he felt no great urgency to make love. What Nell was doing to him was so delightful that there seemed no need to progress to anything else.

Soon her mouth replaced her hands, and she manipulated him with that rare skill Faro remembered so well. Her tongue was like a delicate butterfly trapped within her mouth, stimulating the length of his manhood with its fluttering caresses. Eventually she abandoned his penis, and her active tongue and hands began working their way back up across his stomach and chest. She spread her body over his as she went, and finally ended up as a soft, sensuous presence atop him.

Her kisses tasted like cloves and cinnamon. Faro let his lips stray to her ears and neck, and felt her body tremble with delight in his arms. She moaned softly as his caresses began releasing all the incredible passions of which he knew she was capable. Somehow they managed to wrestle the gown out of the way without abandoning their embrace. Her flesh was warm and soft against his, infinitely desirable as it always had been.

When Faro felt Nell begin shifting to the side, he rolled with her on the bed and ended up in position between her thighs.

"Call me old fashioned," Nell told him softly. "But I still think this way is the best of all."

Faro teased her clit until the warm juices began to flow, then slid neatly into her. She began to come immediately, but Faro knew her well enough to realize that the fun was just beginning. Aroused by her first climax, she demanded more and more of him. Her pelvis rose to meet his thrusts with a rhythm that had always seemed to come naturally for the two of them, and soon he added a few minor variations of movement which he knew would increase the pleasure for both of them.

Nell shuddered into another orgasm, and soon her body was racked by one stirring climax after another. Her head tossed from side to side and her lungs gasped for air as she bucked and shook beneath him. Faro never even considered slowing the pace as his first climax came and went, and his hard dick sent out the message that it was not yet ready to stop either.

Finally when he began to sense that exhaustion was claiming Nell and that she couldn't go on much longer, he released his inner controls and started to come a second time. Nell might or might not have made it with him. By then so many parts of her body were trembling out of control that it was hard to tell.

In deference to their overheated bodies, Faro rolled away onto his back. Nell lay beside him like some sort of victim, her limbs splayed out from her body, unmoving except for the labored rise and fall of her chest.

"Goddamn, Faro!" Nell muttered at last. "I hadn't done any balling like that since . . . hell, it's been so long that I don't even remember when. That sure was somethin'!" Traces of a hillbilly twang were showing up in her speech, a sure indication that she was at ease and contented.

"Come on, Nell," Faro teased her. "You're just trying to make me feel like a big stud or something. I bet you get it that good two or three times a week from these fancy city boys."

"There's plenty here that would like to give it a whirl," she said, "but damned few that can afford my price. In that way, I have come a long ways from my dollar-a-throw Arkansas days. I let my girls carry the load now, but if any fool comes along who wants to cough up some serious folding money for a trip upstairs with me, I sure won't send him on down the street."

Nell rolled on her side and raised up until she could look at Faro. Sweat glistened on her upper lip and her hair hung around her face in ravished disarray. There was an expression on her face unlike any Faro could ever remember seeing there. Gone was the look of the cocky whore, the shrewd businesswoman or the sophisticated lady. She looked vulnerable and slightly sad.

"But you know something, Faro?" she confided. "I guess the passing years have made me take on some odd notions or something. None of those men, no matter how much hard cash they might have in their pockets, ever finds their way in here. Upstairs maybe, but not in here. This is my place, and there's times when I need for it to be separate from all of that out there."

"But I'm here," Faro said.

"That's right. You are."

Hours later, Faro found Greta in the kitchen at the rear of the house. Nell's cook had fixed her something to eat, and she was sitting alone at a small table on one side of the room dining. Her stare was harsh and her tone judgmental when Faro came in and sat down across from her.

"I can't believe you just abandoned me like that," she hissed at him. "Think what might have happened to me in a place like this!"

"You're perfectly safe here," Faro told her. "I haven't seen him, but I'm sure that somewhere around this place Nell has a man with shoulders as broad as a wagon wheel who makes sure that nobody in this house gets bothered. When we made our deal on the train, I promised to keep you safe, but I didn't promise to babysit you every mile of the way to New Orleans."

"But my God, Faro," Greta exclaimed. "How could I possibly know you would bring me to a *house of ill repute?* It sends chills all through me to think about what's taking place on the second floor of this house at this very moment!"

"What kind of chills does it give you, Greta?" Faro grinned. She had no response to that comment. "Look, woman," he continued. "Why don't you just ease up a little, on yourself and on the rest of us as well. I had a reason for bringing you here, and a damned good one too. I talked to Nell about it a little while ago, and she's agreed."

"I shudder to think what you have in mind."

"It's simple. You're going to become a different woman."

"And what, may I ask, is the matter with the woman I now am?" she snapped.

"Right now, you're about as appealing as an ironing board," Faro told her bluntly. "You dress like a parson's grandma, and an eighty-year-old spinster could do her hair and fix herself up more attractively than you manage to. If anybody's after you, they'll be looking for you as you are now. That's why I've decided it's time for a change." He could tell that his uncomplimentary words had deeply offended Greta, but that was all right. He had used them for their shock value anyway.

"You just think you can use this mess I'm in to say or do anything to me that you want!" Greta said accusingly. She was sniffling now, close to another tearful outburst. "Don't you think I know how I look, how plain I am? All my life I've been this way, but it's still cruel of you to talk to me the way you did. You're not a very nice man, Mr. Blake. You're mean and rude and offensive. But don't think you can force me into doing literally anything for the sake of the money. I do have my limits!"

"Well, when you reach about a hundred thousand dollars worth of limits, you let me know, Greta," Faro told her. "But until then, I'm going to keep my part of the bargain, and you're going to keep yours. Hell, consider it a game of some kind if you want to. I'm not asking you to like what's going on, but surely you can force yourself to tolerate it for just a few more days until we get to New Orleans."

"Perhaps I can," Greta replied, sniffling. "What is it you have in mind?"

"I've talked to Nell about it, and she's agreed. Starting tomorrow, some of the girls are going to outfit you with some different clothes, and they're going to show you a few things about painting your face and doing your hair. If they can make you look like you ought to be trying out for a position here at Nell's, then we'll know they've done their job." A look of mortification flashed momentarily across Greta's features, but she said nothing.

"You've got to realize," Faro continued, "that plenty of men would kill for what you've got in that satchel. When you start fooling around with tens and hundreds of thousands of dollars, you're not playing a kiddie game of hide-and-seek anymore. You've stepped over into the big time, and you've got to do things as well as the big boys do it or you'll get squashed like a bug. Do you understand that, Greta?"

She nodded silently.

"Do you understand that we probably have people after us and that we don't even have a notion of who they are? If they're out there, then we're going to have to assume that they're smart and that they're going to be playing the game for keeps. We can't trust anybody, and we can't allow ourselves even one slipup until we get to where we're going."

"I understand all that, Faro," Greta told him finally. "I truly do. But so many things have been happening so fast. Right now I think I'm more frightened and confused than I've ever been in my life. I don't know what to do anymore."

"There's only one thing you can do, and that's to go on," he told her. "For now, you can stay here, or go up to your room, or do whatever you want. Just don't go outside the house and you'll be all right. I'm going to go out front for a while and have a drink, but I'll be close by. Tomorrow, all you have to do is cooperate with Nell's girls."

Faro left Greta staring down at her plate of food, stripped of her appetite by the sobering lecture he had delivered.

Chapter Seven

Nell was stretched out luxuriously on the bed, barely asleep, but not quite ready to wake up and start the day. The sheet lay in a tangle at the foot of the bed, and Faro lay on his side next to her, studying her face and form.

He wasn't sure how old Nell Garvin was. She had started in this business very young, but she'd been at it for quite a number of years. Thirty-five seemed a close estimate, but no one would have guessed that simply by her appearance. Without a doubt, she was the finest-looking woman in this stable of top-quality females, and considering the various lovelies that Nell had working for her, that was saying a lot.

Nell had been smart. She had treated her whoring as a career, one with goals and objectives just like any other profession. And she had taken good care of herself along the way. That was apparent from what Faro was seeing now.

He would have been hard put to say what he appreciated most about Nell's body. Her skin had a pale amber tone, and the texture of fresh butter just drawn from the churn. Her breasts were full and pliant, with small, pleasing nipples that hardened at the slightest hint of attention. She had the firm, slender waist of a twenty-year-old, and a round, tight rear end which he found it hard to keep his hands off of. The tuft of hair between her legs was a silky blond paradise, and her legs themselves were straight, slender works of art.

Of course there were plenty of women in the world who looked as good as Nell, but what had always set her apart from the others to Faro was her bedroom talents. Making love, she combined all the expertise of an experienced prostitute with the patience and tenderness of a cherished lover. There were more passions locked within her one hundred and some pounds than in any other woman Faro had ever encountered.

She awoke with a smile when Faro began to stroke her face with his fingertips. "That's nice," she crooned softly. "You really have a special touch. What was your name again, cowboy?"

"I forgot which name I used on you last night," he told her.

"That's all right, I guess. Just as long as you didn't forget your promise to take me away from all this and make an honest woman of me. You really do love me truly, and you really do own the biggest ranch in Texas, don't you?"

"You don't think I'd tell you a pack of lies just to get you into bed, do you, honey?"

Innocence and merriment danced in Nell's eyes. Her acting talents would have carried her a long way on the stage. "No, I don't think you'd fool a poor little Arkansas gal like me for any such cruel purposes," she told him sweetly. "If you did, I surely would be so heartbroken that I'd probably take a gun and blow your pecker off!"

They kissed and caressed one another with complete enjoyment, though they never did get around to making love. Their prolonged sessions the previous afternoon and evening had left them satisfied for the time being, and this morning it seemed enough just to enjoy a few peaceful minutes together.

Later, Tessie came in bringing them coffee and sweet rolls. The young maid opened the French doors so the morning breeze could enter, then turned to them with a sweet smile and asked if there was any other service she could provide. She was wearing a uniform similar to the one in which she had greeted Faro and Greta at the door yesterday, and as she made her offer, her eyes seemed to communicate a special message to Faro. That look did not escape Nell's attention.

"You little snip!" Nell said to the maid. "I know what's on your mind!" There was no true anger in her voice. The friendship and understanding between herself and her maid were obvious.

"Why Miss Nell!" the girl exclaimed in a mock display of surprise. "Do you think I'd get caught fooling around with this here fine gentleman of yours?"

"You'd try not to get caught at it," Nell chuckled. "Now you get on back to your work, Tessie, and damnit girl, try to keep your drawers on. You'll give my place a bad reputation if you keep giving it away!"

After the maid was gone, Faro and Nell sat naked

in the middle of the bed enjoying their coffee and rolls. "I told Lula and Roxanne to start to work on your friend this morning," Nell told him. "They said it should be quite a lark."

"It'll surely be a challenge for them," Faro commented.

"You might be surprised, Faro my dear," she said. "Somehow I've got a feeling that underneath that straight hair and all that heavy brown wool, there's more woman than you'd think. Or maybe you've already found out what's under there."

Faro looked over at her and grinned. Jealousy hardly befit a woman in her profession, but occasionally he found it entertaining as long as it didn't get out of hand. He decided not to respond to her insinuation.

"Really, Faro, I have trouble understanding your tastes sometimes," Nell told him, somehow offended by his lack of denial. She got up and slipped on a light dressing gown, then went over and parted the curtains in front of the open doors. "It looks like it's going to be a fine day today," she said.

"Good because I have to be out and about," he said. "I've got some errands to run."

"So do I," Nell replied. "We can ride together in my carriage."

Riding up Union Avenue toward the center of Memphis, Nell was greeted occasionally by men on horseback and in passing buggies, but never by any men who were in the company of ladies. Judging simply by her clothing and the fine black carriage she was riding in, it would have been easy to assume Nell Garvin was a society belle. She had dressed this morning in a powder blue dress with full flowing skirts and a modest neckline, and she carried a lacy parasol which matched perfectly the shade of her gown.

"You've really done well for yourself here in Memphis, Nell," Faro was compelled to note once again. "If a man didn't know better, he'd take you for the wife of a senator or a railroad magnate."

"I've had my chances to become both," she admitted, "but the prospect never did appeal to me. I'd hate the idea of having to spend the rest of my life rubbing shoulders with the stuffy upper crust and letting some old fart have free of charge what I might be getting good money for. I've had it better here than I ever have had it anywhere else before, but after two years I know this isn't the place for me."

"I can't say as how I understand that," Faro replied. "Just look at you. You're dressed like a queen, riding in a big fancy carriage, and I saw last night the kind of money your gentleman callers spend in your place. It seems to me that you couldn't ask for anything more than what you've got right here."

For a moment Nell was silent and pensive. She stared down at the parasol which lay closed in her lap, turning it idly in her fingers. Finally she announced, "I'm selling out, Faro. As soon as I can find a buyer for my house, I'm turning the place over and leaving Memphis."

That announcement was startling enough to Faro, but what she told him next was even more surprising.

"And I'm quitting the business, too," she added. "For good."

Faro just shook his head in amazement.

"You know, Faro," Nell went on. "I've spent

more than half my life either on my back with some stranger jamming his prod into me, or setting other girls up for the same thing. And when you get right down to it, there's no difference whether it's in a mining camp in Montana or a fancy house in Memphis. I'm just tired of it. From now on, I'd like for it to be nothing but pure fun, like it was for us last night."

Faro couldn't think of much to say. Nell Garvin had been a prostitute or a madame for as long as he had known her, and it was hard for him to draw a picture of her ever becoming anything different. But he could understand how enough years in that sort of business could tend to wear a woman down.

"I don't think I told you I've heard from Doc, did I?" Nell asked.

"Doc Prentiss?" Faro exclaimed. "It's been a hell of a long time since I got any news about him. What's the old scoundrel up to these days?"

"He's in the middle of what he calls the 'biggest con of my career,'" Nell announced. "A few months back he ran for the California State Assembly and won a seat for himself. Now he claims he's in tight with all the mucky-mucks out on the coast. Come the next election, he says he might even have a shot at the governor's job!"

"Well I'll be dipped in shit!" Faro laughed. "I wonder if the state can survive that?"

"I guess it just makes sense that an ambitious crook like him would eventually end up in the crookedest game of all," Nell said. "The reason he got in touch with me was to try to persuade me to move back west, back to San Francisco. He made me a business proposition."

"What kind of business?" Faro asked.

"He told me the Arbuckle Hotel is going up for sale, and that with his contacts I could get it for half what it's worth."

"The Arbuckle, huh? I'm impressed," he told her. The last time Faro had been in San Francisco, the Arbuckle had been one of the most successful hotel and casino operations in the city.

"Doc said the Arbuckle's not doing so well now," Nell went on to explain, "but he told me in his letter that with the right owner and the right assemblyman to take care of things politically, it could be turned back into a gold mine."

"You and Doc would make one hell of a team," Faro chuckled.

"I like the idea myself," she said. "Over the years, I've built up a comfortable nest egg for myself in a bank in San Francisco, and this seems like a pretty good way to invest it. But I've still got one problem with the whole thing."

"And what's that?"

"I'd need somebody to help me run the place. I'd need a partner that I could trust not to cheat me out of everything."

"Well, you'd have Doc there," Faro said. "Not many people in this world could trust that larcenous old rogue, but you could, Nell."

"I know, but he couldn't be directly associated with the hotel, not if he stays in politics. It would have to be someone else."

By the look in her eye, it suddenly became clear to Faro what she had on her mind. All this roundabout talk of her giving up her whoring ways and going into the hotel business on the West Coast was leading in only one direction.

"How difficult are you going to make this for me,

Faro?" Nell asked with a trace of irritation in her voice. "You know what I'm trying to say."

"I've got a pretty good idea," he admitted, "but I'm not so clear about my answer. I've never given much thought to owning anything that I couldn't stuff into a suitcase or fold up and put in my pocket."

"This isn't something I'm just bringing up on the spur of the moment," Nell told him. Now that the whole thing was out in the open, she was getting hesitant. "I've given the idea a lot of thought, and I believe we'd make a fine team."

Faro knew her words contained a double meaning, and the suggestion gave him a ridiculous, panicky sort of feeling. Before, when he had recognized Nell's efforts to rope and brand him, he had always known the door to freedom was wide open before him. This time would be different. He would be locked in and committed, and he wasn't sure what he should think about that. But there was one thing of which he was sure.

"My luck's been running piss poor lately, Nell," he told her. "If and when I get Greta delivered safely to New Orleans, I'll have a nice chunk of cash coming, but it still wouldn't be enough to buy into this operation. Even at a bargain price, the Arbuckle's bound to go for at least a hundred and fifty thousand dollars."

"That's about the amount Doc mentioned," Nell admitted. "But Doc's got some money to put into it, and I'm pretty sure I can come up with the rest. He and I could front you to start out with, and you could pay us back out of your share of the profits."

"That stinks like charity," Faro grumbled.

"Damn you and your stupid pride, Faro Blake!" Nell told him angrily. "In all the years that you've known me, how often have you ever seen me pass out charity to anybody?" Tears were gathering in her eyes, but Faro set his jaw and looked away from her.

"Then why?" he asked.

"If you can't figure that one out, mister . . ." Nell's voice trailed off and she turned her head away from him, fighting the urge to cry. "Damn you, Faro!" she repeated, dabbing at her eyes with a hankie.

They rode on in silence for the next few minutes, gazing out opposite sides of the carriage, thinking their own thoughts. This situation threw Faro into more confusion than anything had in a long time.

On the one hand, it occurred to him that any man who refused an offer like this must be either a fool or a glutton for poverty. The Arbuckle Hotel could be a gold mine, and what better woman would there be to share such good fortune with than Miss Nell Garvin?

But it would mean giving up his nomadic gambler's ways, perhaps for good, and settling down in one place with one woman. All of his adult life, those had been prospects which Faro had avoided with zealous dedication. What would it be like in one year, or two, or five? Would Nell become a possessive bitch, or an unresponsive fishwife when she finally had the security of knowing he was committed to her? And how much control would she try to wield over him if the money which set them up in business was mostly hers? The prospects of what the union could become were decidedly unsettling, especially if Faro entered into it as the penniless stepson.

The next time Nell spoke to him, she had regained full control of her emotions. Her voice was as chilly as a November wind.

"I only have two stops to make, and then we can go wherever you wish," she said.

"That's fine, Nell," Faro told her. "And listen, about that other business . . ."

"Don't give it another thought, Mr. Blake," she told him icily. "It was a ridiculous notion from the start, and I regret ever having mentioned it!"

Chapter Eight

They returned to Nell's in time to enjoy an early supper with the girls before the evening's activities began. Nell presided over the meal at the head of the table, with Faro on her right. Eight of the ten women in Nell's employment were also there, and gazing around the table at them, Faro thought that Nell really had gathered together the finest stable he had ever seen. The girls were young, mostly in their early twenties, and there wasn't a loser in the bunch. They chatted gaily as they ate, comparing notes about clothes, their favorite customers, how they planned to spend their days off and other such routine matters.

Nell had partially recovered from her earlier anger, but she still addressed Faro in a stiffly courteous manner which he found irritating. To hell with her, he decided. Things had gone well for him today, and if they proceeded according to plan, he and Greta would be on their way tomorrow afternoon.

Midway through the meal the last two members of Nell's troupe, Lula and Roxanne, came into the dining room. They were giggling between themselves, as if they shared some hilarious secret, and when they stopped near the doorway instead of taking their seats, all eyes turned in their direction.

"It's done," Lula announced to the assembled company.

"We're finished with her," Roxanne said.

Faro knew they must be talking about Greta, but when a young woman appeared in the doorway beside them, it still took him a moment to fully realize whom he was looking at.

The changes that the two prostitutes had worked were remarkable. Greta's brown hair was curled and stylishly arranged, and the two finest features of her face, her high cheekbones and dark, serious eyes, were now accentuated with makeup. Her lips were ruby red and she wore a brown beauty mark low on her left cheek.

But what was even more amazing was the shapely figure which filled out the strapless red dress she wore. Nell had been right when she suggested that Greta might have been suffering more from a lack of taste in clothes than from the essential attractive female attributes. The young bank clerk was noticeably uncomfortable in her alluring satin costume, which probably displayed more bosom than she had ever exposed in public, but Faro thought he also detected a certain gleam in her eye which he had never noticed before.

"I wouldn't have believed it," Faro exclaimed. "You look wonderful!"

Greta's eyes fell on him and she smiled tentatively. "I'm worried that I'll catch my death in this thing," she said, "and I'm sure the front's going to fall down any minute now."

"Don't worry, honey," Nell told her with a maternal smile. "You've got enough to keep it up."

"We took her shopping today and bought her four other outfits," Lula told the others. She and Roxanne found places at the table and began heaping their plates, and a moment later Greta came around and took an empty seat beside Faro.

"You did a fine job with her, ladies," Faro said. "I bet her own mother wouldn't recognize her now."

"And if she did, she probably wouldn't admit to it," Greta noted. She flushed when she realized that Faro's glance had fallen instinctively to her pale upper breasts. She kept her eyes averted from him and endured his interest.

As they finished eating, the girls began to filter out of the room one by one, until finally only Faro, Nell and Greta were left in the dining room. There were a few awkward attempts at conversation, but Faro saw that both women were saying a lot more with their eyes and tones of voice than with any words they spoke.

"I'll be glad to pay your girls for their services," Greta offered. "They spent almost the whole day with me."

"That's not the kind of services my girls expect payment for," Nell replied. "Perhaps someday if any of us decide we'd like to become *respectable,* you can return the favor."

Anger flashed in Greta's eyes. "I would be glad to assist you, Miss Garvin, but that might take more than a day to accomplish."

Sensing a cat fight in the making, Faro interfered quickly to change the subject. "So you've bought some more clothes to take along, have you?" he asked Greta.

"You wouldn't believe everything they picked out for me," Greta said. "I'll have three times the luggage I started out with, even if I leave all my old clothes behind."

"We'll make do," he said. "I haven't had the chance to tell you yet that I've arranged for our transportation on to New Orleans. Tomorrow afternoon we'll board the *Sweet Beaulah* and be on our way again."

"On a steamboat?" Greta asked.

"That's right." By the look in his eye, he tried to let Greta know that he didn't want to discuss the matter in front of Nell.

"You must excuse me now," Nell told them, taking the hint. "We'll be opening soon, and I have to make sure everyone and everything is ready. Tuesday is sometimes a fairly busy night for us."

After she was gone, Greta turned in her chair to face Faro. When she noticed his glance straying down the front of her dress again, she said, "I really wish you'd quit that! You act like you've never seen bosoms before, which I know can hardly be true."

Faro grinned. "But I've never seen yours. Up until twenty minutes ago, the notion scarcely crossed my mind that you even had any."

"Well, your lecherous gawking makes me nervous," she told him impatiently. "Now please explain to me why you decided to travel on a steamboat."

"Because it's so unlikely that we would," Faro explained. "Hardly anybody travels by steamboat these days because it's so slow, and there aren't but half a dozen big boats that even make the run down to New Orleans anymore. If I was after us, I'd be watching the train station, so that's why I chose a steamboat. And besides, I think you'll enjoy it. I know I will."

"That's just wonderful," Greta complained. "Now I'm going to go on a pleasure cruise decked out in a scarlet dress like a two-dollar doxy! What other marvelous experiences besides these do you have in store for me, Mr. Blake?"

"Just one more for the time being," Faro told her. "You need to pick up a new style to fit your new looks, Greta. Tonight I'd like for you to spend some time out front mingling and watching how the girls go about their business."

"Good heavens!" Greta exclaimed. "You are joking, aren't you? You couldn't possibly be serious!"

"Look at it this way, Greta. The men you'll be seeing here tonight are all the types of men you've been dealing with for years . . . lawyers, bankers, merchants and other professional men. The only difference is, you'll be seeing another side of them which you probably didn't know they had. And you'll see how Nell's girls bring that side out and cater to it. It seems to me it couldn't hurt any woman to know a thing or two about that."

"You've led me astray this far, Faro," she told him, "so I suppose it can't hurt to go a little farther. But I'll tell you this. If any one of those men so much as touches me this evening . . ."

"God forbid that a man would ever want to touch you, woman!" Faro snapped at her. "That would surely be a terrible thing, wouldn't it?"

A mockingbird sat on one of the low branches of a massive oak tree, running through its repertoire of chirrups, tweets and whistles. Its singing mingled pleasantly with the chords of a tinkling piano and the light sound of female laughter which drifted out toward Faro through the open veranda doors behind him. The honeysuckle blooming on a hedgerow nearby filled Nell's garden with a delightful scent, and the moonlight glistened on the dew-moistened patches of flowers which decorated the yard.

Faro sat on a low stone bench with a glass of bourbon in his hand and a cheroot in his mouth, feeling good. He was about half drunk, and now none of his problems seemed quite as serious as they had three hours ago. Things happened as they were supposed to, whether or not a person spent a lot of time worrying about them.

A shadow momentarily blocked the light which spilled into the garden from the open doorway and he heard the soft rustle of skirts behind him. He turned and saw Nell Garvin coming toward him across the lawn. Somehow, simply by the manner in which she moved, Faro could tell that she was no longer angry with him. She had been drinking most of the evening and still held a half-filled wine glass in her hand.

"Are you all right out here?" she asked, placing a soft hand on his shoulder.

"I'm fine," he said. "I just came out for some fresh air. It's nice out here. Peaceful, kind of."

Nell settled on the grass at his feet, smiling up at him. Her eyes glistened in the moonlight. "I love my garden. I always wanted a garden of my own like this, but I never had the chance to have one until I moved here. It's the one thing I'll regret leaving."

"So you really are going through with this business of buying the hotel and all?"

"Unless it's sold or I get struck dead before I can make the arrangements," Nell vowed.

"I think that's fine, Nell," he assured her. "I think it's a wonderful idea if it's what you want." He puffed the failing ember at the tip of the cheroot back to life and sent a cloud of smoke drifting up from his lips. He could feel Nell's eyes on him, but waited a moment before glancing down at her. "You've got the right idea, laying down roots and changing with the times," he went on. "The old days are disappearing faster than I care to admit. It makes a man start to feel all the years he's already got under his belt."

"Things are changing and we're both a little older," Nell said, "but there's no use getting so goddamn dramatic about it. The fact is, the good times only stop when you let them. Would it be so awful if you had to give up seeing a different town every week and sleeping with a different woman every other night?"

"Maybe not. But I just have trouble picturing what it would be like," Faro admitted.

"Come with me and find out what it would be like," she offered.

"I can't do that. Not just yet."

"Come with me, Faro," she repeated softly. "The money doesn't matter."

"It always has before, Nell. And six months from now, it would again."

She folded her hands across his knees and laid her head down on them. Faro stroked her hair and stared off into the darkness. The mockingbird sang to them and a breeze brought them a fresh whiff of the honeysuckle's sweet perfume.

"During my life," Nell said, "I've had men swear that they loved me and that they wanted nothing else in the world but to spend the rest of their days making me happy. I've had men offer me fortunes to marry them, and I've had them swear they couldn't go on living if I didn't say 'yes.' But you, Faro Blake, you've never made me any promises, and you've never sworn anything. It makes it hard to understand why now, after all the chances I've had, it should be you I want."

"I don't guess I really understand that myself, Nell," Faro told her.

"Would you run like a scalded hound if you heard the word 'love' come out of my mouth, Faro?" she asked.

"Don't you think we both might be a little jaded to be going on about true love and nonsense such as that?" he replied. As soon as the words were out of his mouth, he regretted having said them. He wondered if, deep down, he might be trying to convince Nell that he wasn't worth loving.

"It happens sometimes, even to hardcases like us," she said softly. Nell rose to her feet and took Faro's hand. She led him toward the rear of the yard, back to a grassy spot behind a small rose garden. The odor of her perfume mingled with the scent of the flowers around them as she turned and entered his arms. Her body melted gently against his, as if that was where it belonged. Their lips came together.

Faro took his time with her, letting his lips linger over her neck and shoulders before his hands began any explorations. Nell was submissive tonight, wanting to be gently conquered by him. She trembled in his arms as he unbuttoned the back of her gown and let the front of the garment fall away, but he knew she was not shivering from the chill of the night air. Her flesh was warm and sensitive to his touch. He finished undressing her with a growing feeling of excitement.

"Just look at you, woman!" Faro said admiringly.

He stepped back slightly to admire her form. Her body was an alabaster work of art in the moonlight, a perfect complement to this peaceful garden setting. She smiled, loving his visual caresses. But she was also eager to get on to other things. She helped him out of his jacket, then loosened his string tie.

With Nell's assistance, it took Faro only a minute to remove his clothes. Then he laid her down on the cool grass and stretched out on the ground beside her. As his mouth covered one of her puckered nipples, his hand traveled down across her smooth belly to the silken thatch between her legs. She gasped as his fingertip grazed her firm, sensitive button of womanflesh, and her pelvis arched up to greet his touch. A moment or two of skillful manipulation was all it took to get her fully aroused.

In the midst of their foreplay, Faro heard an odd sound coming from Nell, and in a moment he realized that she was laughing softly to herself. He paused and raised up slightly to look at her. A broad grin was spread across her features.

"What's the joke?" he asked.

"I just had this funny thought." Nell chuckled. "I got to thinking that if I were to bill you for all the pussy I've given you over the years, you'd be the rest of your life trying to pay the debt."

Faro grinned. "Poor girl. I know it's been a strain on you. A lot of times when you snatched ahold of me and drug me off, I knew it was only because you knew I needed a mercy fuck. It was that damned soft heart of yours getting in the way, Nell, honey."

"It's a curse," she said. "But what's a girl to do when she sees a friend with his tongue dragging in the dust out of desperation? I bet you thought I actually *enjoyed* it all those times."

"You sure did have me fooled," he admitted. "Just like you fooled me tonight. But for the time being, I hope you'll go on pretending."

He leaned his head forward and let his tongue graze the sweet lips of her womanhood, which brought the farcical conversation to an abrupt end. He manipulated her with his mouth until he felt her body begin to quiver with orgasmic delight, then shifted around and eagerly slid his thick erection into her. She had little chance to recover before she began to come again, and for the next few minutes her body convulsed with one shuddering climax after another. Finally, when he could stand it no longer, Faro drew his lungs full of air and let go.

He shot a great rush of hot juices into her, and waves of delight began to flood his entire body. He continued to pump with gleeful abandon until he had milked the experience for all it was worth, then collapsed on top of her in a sweaty, spent heap.

Nell grunted from beneath him. "Are you putting on weight, Faro, or do you just fall harder than you used to? I can't hardly breathe down here."

"Sorry," he mumbled. He mustered all his remaining strength and raised up off of her slightly. The muscles on the insides of his thighs were still trembling from the massive moment of release. When Nell urged him away with a hand against his shoulder, he rolled to the side like a log.

"I've got to get back inside as soon as I cool down a little bit," Nell said. "I really only intended to step outside a minute to tell you something, but then I forgot all about it. It's about your friend."

"Greta? What about her."

"You might want to keep an eye on her. I think she's getting potted."

"Greta's getting drunk?" Faro exclaimed. "Good God! That woman never stops surprising me."

"Well she might surprise herself if you don't watch out for her," Nell said. "She doesn't seem to understand much about drinking champagne."

"I guess I'd better get in there," Faro said, reaching tiredly for his clothes. "If anything happens to her tonight, she'll sure as hell blame me for it in the morning!"

Only four of Nell's girls remained in the front parlor when Faro reentered the house. They were entertaining the last couple of male visitors with drinks and invitations, but the hour was getting late and business was slow. Faro immediately thought the worst when he didn't spot Greta anywhere in the room. There would be hell to pay if she woke in the morning and realized she had been violated the night before by one of Nell's customers.

Roxanne was sitting on a couch across the room, enduring the drunken fondlings of an old man in an expensive gray suit. When she saw Faro glancing around, she pointed toward a small alcove which was separated from the rest of the parlor by brocade curtain. Faro went over to the alcove and pulled the curtain back slightly to investigate.

Greta was sitting in the lap of a handsome young man of thirty. She had one arm around his shoulders and held a full champagne glass in her other hand. She was smiling broadly and drunkenly. She seemed oblivious to the fact that her skirts and petticoats were gathered in a wad in her lap and that her companion's hand was making steady progress up the inside of her thigh.

The man was not nearly so drunk as Greta. He

scowled at Faro, obviously irritated by the interruption. It took Greta a little longer to acknowledge Faro's presence.

"Faro, my bodyguard!" Greta exclaimed in a thick-tongued slur. Then, turning to her companion, she explained, "You know, I'm paying him to guard my body from people like you, Harold."

"That's Gerald," the man grumbled.

"Harold is a banker too," Greta told Faro brightly. "We've been in here discussing fiduciary matters." She spoke like her mouth was filled with marbles and her tongue didn't have room to operate properly.

"Are you really her bodyguard?" the young man asked. "She told me she was just a visitor here, but I thought that maybe . . ." He wasn't too sure what he had gotten himself into.

"I'm more of a traveling companion," Faro explained. "Greta isn't a regular here, and you'd probably be better off with one of the other girls."

"That's beginning to sound like a good idea," the other man admitted.

There was an awkward moment as he tried to get out from under Greta, but as soon as he was able he left the alcove while Faro remained to attend to his limber charge. Greta plopped back limply into the chair, but Faro was able to get her to her feet and support her with an arm around her back. He started across the parlor, half leading her and half carrying her.

"You know what I did?" Greta asked in a conspiratorial giggle. As they started up the stairs her feet went out from under her and they nearly went down, but Faro regained control of her in time.

"I can't imagine," Faro said.

"I let him feel my bosoms," she announced. "It wasn't so bad, either."

"Some women actually like that sort of thing, Greta."

"I've had my bosoms touched before, you know, Faro," she told him. "This wasn't the first time for me. But this time it felt good. Do you think it could be because of the champagne?"

"That just might have something to do with it."

They made steady progress down the second floor hall, and when they reached Greta's room, Faro led her over to the bed and let her fall across it. "He kissed me, too," she admitted wickedly. "While we were talking about fiduciary something or another. He kissed me and he touched my bosoms back there in that little room. . . ." Her voice was trailing away and her eyelids were losing their battle to remain open. Faro found a blanket at the foot of the bed and spread it over her. By the time he eased out the door and shut it behind him, she was already beginning to snore.

Greta spent all of the next morning in her room. Late in the morning Faro sent Tessie up with some coffee, and when the maid reported back to him, she confirmed his suspicions. Greta was paying the awesome toll for her riotous activities. He decided that the soundest policy was to leave her alone until she recovered.

After lunch Faro and Nell took a ride in her carriage, and when they returned a couple of hours later, Greta was up and around. Faro went up to check on her, and he soon discovered that being in the same room with her was like trying to share a den with a wolverine. Her face was pallid beneath the layer of makeup the girls had helped her apply, and the only thing that kept her temperament from being explosive was the pounding in her head every time she raised her voice.

"I guess I should have warned you about that champagne," he said, trying to conceal his amusement, "but I saw that it was relaxing you and I didn't realize you were putting away so much of it."

Greta tossed a dark look in his direction as she continued packing her belongings into a suitcase. "My memories are a little fuzzy about the last part of the night," she confessed.

"Maybe it's just as well," Faro chuckled. She scowled at him again and laid a second suitcase on the bed beside the first. She had also bought some new luggage the day before in which to carry her additional clothing.

"I'm sending you ahead by yourself to board the *Sweet Beaulah*," Faro told her. "I don't want it to look like we're traveling together, but our cabins are near each other and I'll be closeby on the boat in case you run into trouble. The name you'll use on the boat is Grace Worthington."

Greta surprised him by answering simply, "That's fine." She was apparently too miserable to argue with him at the moment.

"Where's the satchel?" he asked.

"Oh, I didn't tell you, did I? Since that man on the train already got a look at what I was carrying it in, I switched the money to a new container." She reached under the bed and produced a small leather briefcase, which she laid on the bed. Faro opened it and briefly ogled the stacks of bills inside before closing it again.

"I don't suppose you'd consent to let me carry that," he said.

"I see no need for it," Greta told him. "If my disguise is as good as you claim, then the money should be fine with me. Besides, you know I'll be on that steamboat, but if I went ahead and left the money behind with you . . ." She laid the briefcase inside one of her suitcases and folded a dress on top of it. Faro decided not to debate.

"The trip downriver will take about four days," Faro told her. "Once we get settled in, I think you'll enjoy yourself, and you're really not in all that big a hurry to get to New Orleans anyway, are you?"

"I suppose not. It will be at least another week before Anthony arrives, and maybe longer if any complications have arisen in St. Louis." Greta closed the filled suitcase and fastened the leather straps which held it shut. Then she turned to Faro and added, "Actually, the more I think about it, the better I like this idea of traveling by steamboat. As a matter of fact, several of your ideas are making more sense to me now than they did when you came up with them. I'm finally starting to get a feeling that things are going to be all right for us."

"That's good news," Faro said. "When you've finished packing, call me and I'll help you get your baggage downstairs. Nell's carriage is waiting outside to take you to the levee, and I'll be along about thirty minutes after you board the boat."

After he saw Greta off, Faro went out to the small gazebo in the side yard where Nell sat drinking tea. She poured him a cup and sweetened it with honey for him, then sat back in her chair studying him. Faro sipped his tea and stared down the peaceful, tree-lined street. He wasn't quite as confident as Greta that they would encounter no more trouble on the second leg of their journey, and he felt at this moment as if he was leaving some sort of sanctuary to reenter once more the real, and dangerous, world.

"Thanks for not asking a lot of damned questions about this business with Greta and me," Faro told Nell.

"All my life I've had so many problems of my own that I guess there never was much time left for butting into other people's affairs," she said. "After a while, I guess it gets to be a habit."

"But you were still curious, I bet."

"She was such a queer sort, I was curious about whether you'd spiked her or not," Nell admitted. "I figure if there's any man talented enough to get inside that woman's lead-lined bloomers, it's probably you."

"One of your customers almost got in last night," Faro chuckled, "and I guess I could have. But I had you waiting."

"Don't count on that always being the case, though, Faro. I don't plan to dry up and blow away passing the time while you get the itch out of your britches. By the time you get around to making up your mind, it could be too late."

"I know that, Nell. We'll just have to wait and see, I guess."

"I guess we will," Nell said, but she was smiling one of those secret female smiles, as if she already knew what the future would bring.

Chapter Nine

Faro Blake's first glimpse of the steamboat *Sweet Beaulah*, tied off against the levee of the sprawling Mississippi, carried him back almost thirty years. He could recall quite clearly the first day he ever stepped aboard such a vessel and began learning the profession that would eventually become his life's work.

He had been ten years old at the time, still reeling from his mother's death during a cholera epidemic, and none too sure how he should feel about being uprooted from the rural Kentucky countryside which had always been his home. They had told him that he was going to join his father, a riverboat gambler on the Mississippi, but beyond that he had no notion about what sort of life lay in his future.

It had taken him a while to warm up to A. B. Blake. Living fatherless for the first ten years of his life had instilled a certain bitterness in Faro, even though he soon came to realize that A. B. had not known he had had a son at all. But despite the gypsy ramblings that A. B.'s profession demanded, he dedicated himself to fatherhood. Eventually a strong bond formed between the two of them.

Doc Prentiss had also been a major influence on Faro's life during those early days. Not only had he undertaken the task of providing Faro with the basics of an education, but he had also tried to impart to the youth a practical knowledge of the world they lived in. Though Doc was by choice a con man rather than a gambler, it was from him instead of from his father that Faro began to learn the skills of a professional gambler.

A. B. had high aspirations for his son and shunned the idea of Faro following in his footsteps. When Faro was eighteen, his father sent him off to attend the University of Louisiana. But eight years of migrant steamboat life had instilled in Faro a restless spirit which made college seem like prison. Within a few short months he was expelled from school for gambling and had set out to pattern his life after that of his father. After plying his trade during the war on both sides of the battle lines, Faro served a brief prison sentence for smuggling before being lured west by the promise of excitement and wealth in the bustling frontier regions of North America. He had been at it ever since, and seldom had he regretted the nomadic and adventuresome way of life he had chosen.

The *Sweet Beaulah* looked shabby indeed compared to the glittering river palaces which Faro had once called home. Her peeling decks and woodwork were in desperate need of scraping and paint, and her brass fittings had long since tarnished to dull shades of brown and sickly green. A handful of laborers were at work on the main deck of the boat, moving cargo lethargically from one place to another and tending to the two large boilers. Only a scattering of passengers wandered the second deck, and the texas and pilothouse above seemed abandoned. Before the war, the Memphis levee had been a teeming center of commerce and an embarcation point for hundreds of travelers each week, but now it lay stark and empty, populated primarily by derelicts and wharf rats.

Nobody questioned Faro as he crossed the main walkway to board the boat, but a smiling black steward in a starched white jacket greeted him as he mounted the stairs to the passenger deck. The steward showed him to his quarters and informed him that only about twenty-five passengers were booked for the downriver trip.

The cabin to which Faro was assigned was similar in size and configuration to the train compartment he had been in a few days before. There was a narrow bed, storage space for his valise and case of gambler's accessories, and a small table with a single wooden chair. One door entered the compartment from the outside, and a second opposite the first opened into the passenger dining room which ran lengthwise down the center of the passenger deck.

After stowing his luggage, Faro peeled out of his jacket and vest and lay down on the bed, deciding to postpone any explorations of the boat. Though the chance was slight, somebody might be watching the levee, and it would be better if he remained out of sight until they were under way.

Even this inadequate replica of the grand side-wheelers on which he and his father once lived brought a host of memories flooding back—smelling the thick rich aroma of expensive cigars, hearing the crisp snap as a new deck of cards was shuffled by expert hands, feeling the rising tension in the air as cards were dealt and the pot grew, watching with elation as his father casually raked in hundreds of dollars on a winning hand.

When he was twelve, he had seen his father kill a man during a dispute over a hand of cards. The derringer had appeared in A. B.'s hand as if by magic, and in the wink of an eye a Mississippi planter four feet away was slumped dead across the green felt table, his lifeless fingers still clutching the small revolver he had been trying to draw. It was the first time Faro had ever seen how suddenly and violently death could strike, and every detail of the incident had been recorded indelibly on the canvas of his memory.

Without warning, the steamboat shuddered, as if racked by a minor explosion somewhere below, but Faro felt no alarm. The first jolt was followed by a series of lesser quakes and the growing thunder of heavy machinery being called into service. Faro rose from his bed and glanced out a small window in time to see the levee sliding slowly away from the hull of the steamboat. They were under way at last.

Dusk spread a golden sheen across the broad, rolling surface of the river. Standing along the railing on the starboard side of the passenger deck, Faro stared across the mile or so of churning floodwaters which separated Tennessee from Arkansas. He marveled, as he had countless times before, at the indomitable spirit of the great Mississippi. Within Faro's lifetime, men had already commenced feeble efforts to dictate her channel and direction of flow, but she refused to be tamed so easily. When the spring runoffs swelled the river, she could still be as whimsically powerful as any of nature's wonders. In the course of a few minutes she could alter her channel dramatically, lopping off dozens of square miles of land from one bank and attaching it to the other, heedlessly consuming farms, fields and occasionally entire towns.

Noticing a movement on the deck to his right, Faro turned his head in that direction, and for a moment he could not keep himself from staring. Greta Wimbley was strolling down the deck toward him, smiling gaily as she chatted with the man walking beside her. She held his arm in a surprisingly familiar manner, and Faro noticed immediately that she had changed into a blue satin gown as seductively low cut as the one she had worn the night before at Nell Garvin's.

Faro immediately disliked the man she was with. He was handsome in a slick, superficial way, and as they talked, his eyes scanned Greta's face and form with shallowly concealed appetite. He was dressed in a tight-fitting striped suit and on his head a fashionable derby sat at a jaunty angle. As the couple strolled past, the man touched the brim of his hat to Faro in casual greeting, and Faro responded with a quick, impersonal nod. Greta did not acknowledge his presence in any way, but continued her light conversation with her companion.

"I find your line of work *soo* interesting, Mr. Kelso," she said loudly enough for Faro to overhear. "Imagine traveling all over the country making your living as a salesman!"

"Selling beautiful clothing to beautiful ladies such as yourself has many rewards besides the obvious financial ones," the man pointed out.

"I'm sure it does," Greta tittered as they passed

out of sight around a corner. Her manner was a precise mimicry of one of Nell's whores.

"A goddamn drummer!" Faro grumbled to himself as he turned back to the rail. "That figures."

It was almost dark by the time the steward made a tour of the deck inviting the passengers to dinner. In the dining room, Faro chose a seat as far away as possible from Greta and her new friend, then concentrated on keeping his eyes from straying in their direction.

Some efforts had been devoted to keeping the dining room luxurious in the best riverboat tradition. Three sparkling chandeliers hung above the long oak table, and the china and silverware at the place settings bore the crest of the steamboat line which owned the *Sweet Beaulah*. The meal of roast beef, potatoes, carrots and stewed apples was hot and delicious, and the black steward did his best to provide adequate service to his twenty-five charges.

Faro found himself seated next to a portly, middle-aged cotton broker from Memphis who divided his time between dripping gravy down the front of his shirt and bemoaning the elimination of slavery nearly twenty years before. Faro soon discovered that an occasional grunt or nod was all that was required to sustain his end of the conversation.

The other diners were mostly men, and from the tone of the various conversations around the table, Faro guessed that the majority of his fellow passengers were on their way to New Orleans for business reasons. In addition to Greta, there were two elderly women who seemed to be traveling together and kept mostly to themselves, and a lovely young woman of about twenty in the company of a boyish youth of the same age. From the cow-eyed gazes which they constantly exchanged, it was obvious that they were honeymooners, or at least lovers. The prospects of finding any entertaining way in which to pass his time on board the steamboat seemed remote.

From the look of things, Greta was not experiencing the same problem at the far end of the table. A young officer from the boat, probably a pilot or a first mate, was steadily encroaching on the territory which Kelso, the drummer, had already staked out, and Greta was also drawing interested stares from a number of other men around the table.

It amused Faro to watch Greta reveling in such attention. For a young woman who had spent so much of her life as a drab, neglected spinster, this must all be as new and intoxicating as a visit to a foreign land. She did her best to divide her chattering conversation between her two main admirers, while still spreading her smiles around the table to all the other men who seemed to be eager to receive them. There was very little about her now which resembled the austere, vindictive wench who had snarled and snapped at him so recently through the connecting doors of their train compartments.

But Faro also felt a paternal sort of jealousy when he realized how vulnerable Greta would be to the wiles and seductions of her attentive admirers. He had not forgotten how near to sexual capitulation a few glasses of champagne had carried her the night before at Nell's, and the wine was flowing no less freely at her end of the table tonight. It might serve them both well if he kept a pretty close eye on her for the remainder of the evening. Playing a part was one thing, and stumbling into the bed of the first charmer who was clever enough to get her drunk beyond the point of restraint was quite another.

After dinner, Faro carried the brandy which the

steward served him out onto the open observation area at the fore of the passenger deck. Soon most of the other passengers had also left the dining room to stroll around the deck or return to their cabins, but Greta remained inside with a core of admirers surrounding her. Occasionally, he heard her tittering laughter filtering out through the open doors and glanced around in alarm, realizing that she was getting drunk again. But there was nothing he could do about it at the moment except stay close in case things got out of hand. Most of the time he kept his gaze fixed out across the open water, watching the lights on the bank float by through the darkness.

At last when the boredom became oppressive, Faro decided to take a stroll around the deck. Only a few lights shone in the windows of the cabins he passed, and the peaceful atmosphere which prevailed on board the boat struck him as strange and slightly depressing. For want of any better way to pass the time, he decided that he would turn in as soon as he was sure Greta had returned safely to her cabin.

When he returned to the front portion of the deck, he could tell that a few people were still gathered inside, but a moment later when he glanced in, he realized that Greta was not among them. The chair where she had presided over her admirers was vacant, and the bottle of wine which she and Kelso had been sharing was gone. It was no surprise to see that Kelso had also disappeared.

It was ridiculous to feel any sort of concern, Faro decided. Chances were the drummer had simply walked her to her cabin before returning to his own quarters for the night. But even if Greta had invited her companion to stop by for a nightcap, or for something even more intimate, what concern was it of his? She and Faro had a business arrangement, and if he did not permit her to dictate to him any code of morality, how could he then tell her what her personal conduct should be? But in a minute he still found himself marching down the outside walkway toward her compartment.

No light shone through the curtained window of Greta's cabin, and when he pressed his ear against the door, he couldn't detect any sounds inside. He tried the doorknob and found it locked. He knocked lightly, but received no answer.

Light footsteps alerted him to someone's approach. Faro turned as if he was simply headed down the walkway toward his own door, but he was a second late with his reaction. Greta stopped about twenty feet away at the end of the walkway and stared into the darkness toward him. "Who's there?" she asked guardedly.

"It's me, Greta," he told her in a hushed tone. "Where in the world have you been?"

"What business is that of yours?" Greta asked as she started toward him.

"Look, you need to watch yourself with that drummer," Faro advised her as she stopped beside him. She took her key out of her reticule and stuck it in the lock. "I've seen his type a hundred times before, and I know he's up to no good."

Greta opened her door a few inches, but made no move to ask him in. "It's late, Faro," she told him. "It's been a long day, and I'm very tired."

"I think we need to have ourselves a talk," he told her. He shoved the door open and entered without invitation. With a resigned sigh, Greta followed him in, then closed the door behind her. Faro struck a lucifer and lit the lamp which hung on the wall by the door.

"I think you just want to check around and make sure I haven't got a man hidden under my bed," Greta accused. "I saw those looks you were giving me at dinner. What's gotten into you anyway?"

"Damnit, nothing's gotten into me!" Faro growled. "It's just that I'm supposed to be watching out for you, and you're not helping things a bit with the way you've been flouncing around like a goddamn bitch in heat. Where did you go with that damn drummer, anyway?"

"I wasn't even with Mr. Kelso," Greta told him angrily. "If you *must* know, Mr. Locke took me up to see the pilothouse. It was all perfectly respectable, and we couldn't have been gone more than ten minutes."

"I see," Faro said. By then he was beginning to recognize his own jealousy, which only increased his anger.

Greta hung the lace shawl she had been wearing inside her cabin's small closet, then sat down on the edge of the bed. The lamplight gave her pale skin a delicate ivory tone, and as she leaned forward to slip off her shoes, Faro realized how truly revealing her dress was to a man with the proper vantage point. Sitting beside her all through dinner, Kelso must have had trouble keeping his tongue from hanging out of his mouth.

"What has gotten into you, Faro?" she asked him again.

"What's gotten into me!" he exclaimed. "Just look at you, woman! Your tits are fairly falling out the front of that dress, and our first night on board you start acting like you'd love to make every male passenger under sixty and half the crew to boot!"

Greta rose from the bed and turned to face him directly. An unexpected smile began to dissolve the lines of anger from her face as she said, "This morning when I got up I was still wearing that red dress, and when I walked in front of a mirror, I thought for an instant that somebody else was in the room with me. All of a sudden it struck me like a lightning bolt that that was me, and that I was pretty. *For the first time in my life, I was truly pretty!* Can you imagine what a discovery that was to a woman like me?"

"It was quite a change," Faro concurred.

"All my life, I've been plain and dreary," she went on. "I had seen other women paint their faces and wear pretty clothes, but it had never occurred to me that such things could make any difference in the way I looked. I guess I've always hated pretty women simply because they were pretty. Men paid attention to them, but a thousand times in my life I've seen men's eyes pass right over me as if I wasn't there. But tonight, out there in the dining room . . . you saw how it was. I looked like a different woman, and I acted like a different woman. *I was a different woman!*"

"What in the hell have I done?" Faro asked in wonderment.

"You've done me the most marvelous favor that anyone ever has!" Greta told him brightly. "And I can hardly believe that I fought you every step of the way." She laid one of her suitcases up on the bed and began taking out her night clothes as she talked. Faro discovered that her new wardrobe even included some frilly new bedwear. "I'm not going to be a bit of trouble to you for the rest of the trip," Greta promised him. "We're safe here aboard the boat, so you can go your way without worrying about me. For the first time in my life, I'm going to have myself some fun!"

"Good God," Faro mumbled darkly.

"I really do need to get some rest now, Faro," Greta told him. "I've drunk more wine these last two days than I ever have in my life, and I'm exhausted. But thanks for your concern, and thank you very much for making me go with you to Miss Garvin's."

By the time he reached the door of his own cabin, Faro was still shaking his head in amazement. He had expected practically anything to happen but this, and now that he had witnessed the full effects of his handiwork, he could only speculate in what sizzling directions Greta's quest for "fun" might lead her. He decided that all he could do was stay close by and watch what happened. He had a notion that in the hands of the right suitor, she might easily be confronted with more "fun" than she really cared to deal with.

Floating in a drowsy, nether realm just before sleep claimed him that night, Faro found himself recalling the sensuous vision of two pale, gently rounded breasts straining at the fabric of a light blue dress which scarcely concealed them.

Chapter Ten

Faro passed most of the next morning idly in his cabin, and after lunch he accepted an invitation to play in a small-stakes poker game one of his fellow passengers was putting together. Giles Pounders, the cotton broker who sat next to Faro at dinner the previous evening, had gathered together half a dozen men with a few extra dollars in their pockets, and they assembled at a felt-covered, eight-sided table at one end of the dining room.

After thirty minutes of play, Faro realized that the game was going to be about as interesting as pitching pennies at a cup, but he stayed on because he was winning a few dollars at a time and the game was slightly less boring than doing absolutely nothing. Despite what Pounders considered his own aggressive betting style, the pots seldom ranged higher than twenty dollars, and at the end of four hours of play, Faro discovered that he had gained a little less than one hundred dollars for a whole afternoon of effort. Still, though, it felt good to have even such a bankroll lining his pockets again.

At the dinner table that evening, Faro watched with vague disgust as Kelso scrambled for his usual seat at Greta's left, capturing that place of distinction over the efforts of two other rivals. The pilot named Locke occupied the seat on her right, which seemed to be his customary place, and next to him sat the elderly captain at the far end of the long table. Faro again found himself in the droll company of Pounders, whose obsessive choice of mealtime topics this evening was why the railroads were destroying the South.

They dined on roast pork and cornbread, and after dinner Faro stayed on for cigars and brandy with several of the other men. The talk turned, as it so often still did south of the Mason–Dixon line, to a rehash of how the Confederacy had nearly won the war, and for the next hour Faro listened with minimal interest as one man after another lauded himself for his great feats of bravery during the conflict. Faro kept his mouth shut. Even when the war was going on, he had considered the whole thing a waste of lives and lead, and now, nearly twenty years later, he hadn't changed his opinion.

Greta had disappeared outside with the drummer shortly after the meal was over, but Faro was determined tonight not to interfere in her affairs. Still, though, he couldn't help mulling over the situation. He couldn't really imagine what she saw in Kelso, but if she was just out to practice her new-found charms on somebody and, as she had said, have some fun, then he supposed the slick-mannered traveling salesman would serve as well in that capacity as any other man aboard the *Beaulah*. She had assured him that she was a grown woman and that she was capable of making her own choices. If she chose to explore the delights of sexual congress with one or a dozen men on board the boat, what concern was that of his? That was her business, hers and the man's she was with. Right now that was between her and Kelso.

The hell it was!

The other men at the table watched with surprise as Faro rose suddenly from his chair and stomped out of the dining room. He marched down the walkway with a determined stride, not pausing an instant to consider what he was doing. He could feel an irrational fury rising within him toward the drummer, and the feeling only seemed to increase as he drew closer to Greta's cabin door.

Making no pretense of knocking, Faro flung the door open, then swept the interior of the cabin with a searing glare.

"What the hell?" Kelso grumbled, glancing toward Faro in surprise. Greta sat on the edge of the bed with her skirts bunched up above her knees, and the drummer was kneeling before her. For an instant, Faro thought he must either be about to propose or to commence some bizarre sex act. Then he realized what was really going on. Several pairs of hosiery lay on the floor beside Kelso, and he held a sheer black stocking bunched up at one of Greta's feet.

"What are you doing here?" Greta demanded immediately. "Can't I have any privacy?"

"You mean you know him, Grace?" Kelso asked her. A look of uncertainty and rising fear was beginning to replace the anger on his face as he glanced from one to the other.

Faro's furious stare did all his communicating for him.

"We're traveling together, but that's all," Greta said.

"Look, pal. I was just . . ." the drummer began to stammer. "I mean, this here, it wasn't . . ." He was hurriedly cramming hosiery in his pocket, desperate to make the evidence disappear. Faro neither moved nor spoke.

"You don't have to explain anything to him!" Greta insisted. "I can do anything I want with whomever I want!"

"Yeah, but you didn't tell me that you and him was . . . together!"

When Faro vacated the doorway for an instant, Kelso dashed through it like a hare with a hound nipping at his tail. As his hurried footsteps faded down the walkway, Faro stepped into the cabin and closed the door behind him. Greta remained seated on the bed with a white stocking on her left leg and a black one gathered around the toe of her right foot.

"Playing dress-up?" Faro asked.

"He was seducing me, you dolt!" Greta told him with cold disdain. "He told me he just wanted to show me some samples of his merchandise, but I'm not stupid. I knew what he was up to."

"What was supposed to come next? Garter belts and fancy bloomers?"

"You know what would have come next if you hadn't burst in here like you did!" she stormed. "What right have you?"

"Goddamn, woman!" Faro shouted. "What all did those girls back at Nell's teach you besides how to dress and fix yourself up?"

"Perhaps I've been learning from your example,

Mr. Blake! What's the difference between what you did with that little doxy on the train and what I was about to do here?"

There was no difference. Suddenly Faro began to realize what a ludicrous thing he had done.

"What is it, Faro?" Greta asked. "Were you jealous? Do you want me for yourself?"

"That must be it," he admitted.

A look of satisfaction spread across Greta's face. "Finally!" she exclaimed.

She had a small pink birthmark low on her abdomen. It was shaped almost exactly like a miniature pair of lips, and a single black hair grew out of the center of it. Strange, Faro thought.

Greta's body was somehow leaner than he had expected it to be. Her waist was slender and firm, and her hips were almost boyishly narrow. He had no complaints, however, about the sleek perfection of her legs, nor the soft fullness of her breasts. Her flesh had an unusual pallid cast to it which he found alluring.

An air of tension and a decided lack of spontaneity had permeated their attempt at lovemaking. Despite her expressed desire to go through with it, she had begun to stiffen as soon as he started to undress her. Thirty minutes of gentle caresses and soft reassurances relaxed her to a degree, but she froze up again the moment he penetrated her. The act had suddenly become mechanical and unfulfilling, and Faro gave up his efforts before either of them derived any satisfaction from it.

Greta lay on her back beside him now, unmoving, staring up at the ceiling of the cabin. The light from a candle across the room danced in her expressionless eyes. She could have been a corpse, except for a single tear which lay glittering on her cheek.

"Why?" she asked finally.

Faro considered the question for a moment, then finally whispered, "Why what?"

"I don't know," she said. "Right now a thousand questions are running through my head, and I don't have answers for any of them. I wanted to make love, to *really* make love with you, so why couldn't I? Before a week ago, I had never stolen a single thing in my entire life, so why did I suddenly agree to steal one hundred thousand dollars from the bank I worked for? Why am I going to New Orleans to meet a man I care so little about? Why is my life changing so suddenly from the way it's always been?"

"I can't answer any of those questions for you," Faro said. "But you will have to admit one thing. Things sure haven't been boring for you lately, have they?"

"Certainly not."

"Maybe you're just afraid because for the first time in your life, you're letting go. You're discovering what life is about beyond your two-room walk-up and your cubbyhole at Fidelity Trust."

"Change has always frightened me," Greta said. "And the changes which are going on inside me right now are downright terrifying. I have no idea where it's all going to lead me to."

Faro sat up on the edge of the bed and fished in his jacket for a cheroot, then lit it over the candle flame. He wasn't all that insensitive to Greta's dilemma, but he did realize where all this deep discussion was likely to lead—nowhere. Most of the time, people simply did what they did. Their insides were their boss, and reason seldom had anything to do with it.

Greta reached out her fingers to stroke his back, and Faro was surprised to detect real tenderness in her touch. "I'm sorry about the way things happened," she told him. "Ever since that first night on the train, I imagined it all completely different. I just don't have much experience with men."

"It takes time," Faro assured her.

"When I was fifteen," she said, "my mama sat me down one time and told me all she knew about this sort of thing. She said that after I was married, about once a week my husband would want to put it in me. She told me I always had to let him, or else he might go out to some saloon somewhere and maybe catch a filthy disease. But with you . . . I keep feeling like you wanted to give me something, and not just take it."

"That's about right," Faro said. He turned and gave her a soft kiss, then drew back a few inches to study the features of her face. "We won't be together long enough for me to teach you much," he told her.

"But . . ." she suggested.

"But we haven't reached New Orleans yet, have we?"

"There's a little time," Greta agreed.

Faro stubbed out his cigar and stretched out on the bed beside her once more. "The main thing is just to relax," he said. "No matter what I do to you, all you have to think about is whether or not it feels good. And if it feels good, then just let your body flow with it. The minute you start to worry about what your mama said or whether or not you'll go to hell if you do it, I guarantee you the fun's over. Now relax."

Greta closed her eyes, and in a moment a comfortable smile crept across her lips. Faro let his kisses roam over her cheeks, across her eyes, and back to her mouth again. Her breathing was smooth and regular, and her smile never faded. His fingers were gently massaging the smooth flesh of her arm, and when his forearm brushed across her nipple, she didn't flinch. She began to sigh softly as his lips wandered across her ear and down the side of her neck.

"It feels nice, Faro," she whispered. "I didn't know my skin was so sensitive."

"It gets better."

When he thought she was ready, he started down across her throat with his mouth and tongue, taking his time, making sure his advance across each inch of unexplored territory was made with the utmost tenderness. When he reached the nipple of her right breast it was standing up firmly, eager to receive his attention. His tongue delicately sampled its shape and texture before his lips finally closed over it. Greta's fingers laced themselves through his hair and she moaned quietly.

He could feel her body begin to come truly alive. Every place that his hands wandered increased her delight, and when his fingertips finally began to explore up the inside of her thigh, her legs parted wider in spontaneous invitation. She winced with pleasure as his finger traced the perimeters of her womanhood and grazed briefly across her clitoris. Before, when he had touched her there, she had turned to wood beside him.

In a moment, Greta raised up in slight alarm and asked, "What's that wetness?"

"It's from you," Faro said. "It's supposed to happen."

"But it never did before with . . ."

"With Anthony Winchell?" Faro chuckled. "For some reason I suspected the two of you had probably hooked up at one time or another."

"Since we were going to get married, I didn't think I wanted him going out and catching some filthy disease," she replied lightly, relaxing back on the pillow. "But now I'm not so sure which would have been worse."

Greta's breath began to quicken as Faro concentrated his attention on the most sensitive areas of her body. Slowly he began to abandon some of his former caution as she surrendered herself more completely to the experience. Sweat began to bead up on her body and her head tossed from side to side erratically. Her moans were chesty demands for more and more of the same.

Finally Faro decided the time was right and plunged his finger deep within her. Greta's eyes opened wide with sudden alarm and her body stiffened like a steel rail. "My God! What was that?" she gasped.

"What was what?"

"It felt like what you did sent a spark way up inside me. It was strange."

"Was it good?" Faro asked. By her attitude, he could tell that the erotic moment was past for her. But at least she had gotten a taste of the delicious finish she was meant to enjoy.

"It felt good, but it was such a surprise," she said. "I thought something had gone wrong down there."

"The only thing wrong was that it didn't last longer." Faro chuckled. "But don't worry. The next time it will be a little better, and the time after that, still better. I guess lesson number one is over for now."

"And what about this?" Greta asked, looking down at his thick erection and touching it tentatively.

"Unless I miss my bet," Faro said, "that will figure prominently in lesson number two."

Faro returned to his own cabin for the night, but after breakfast the next morning he found his student eager to return to the classroom. Once they were alone in her cabin, Greta shed her clothing with immodest zeal, then lay down on the bed to wait for him to finish undressing.

"What's the rush, anyway?" Faro asked her with a laugh.

"I had this dream last night," she explained. "About us. And then this morning when I woke up, I had this funny feeling all over. It felt like . . . well . . . like I wished you and I were already in bed together."

"In some circles," Faro explained with a laugh, "that is referred to as being 'horny.'"

"Well I liked it, but it sure would be a problem if it happened every morning. All through breakfast, I couldn't seem to think about anything but what would happen during lesson two. Hurry up, will you?"

The heat in the cabin and their own rising temperatures made their union a slippery, but rewarding experience. After her erotic dream, Greta was more easily aroused this morning, and Faro found her quim damp with anticipation when he finally got around to slipping his eager member into her. Because of the two unrewarding sessions the night before, he decided it was his turn this morning, and after no more than two minutes of dedicated effort, he found himself groaning and writhing like a madman as his accumulated frustrations gushed from his body.

They passed the morning in their exhaustive study. When Faro finally came from her cabin shortly before noon, his sated grin was as broad as a skillet. He returned directly to his cabin, stripped down to bare skin and collapsed across his bed.

Chapter Eleven

Faro sat in the chair in Greta's cabin with his feet propped up on the edge of the bed. A glass and a half-empty bottle of bourbon sat on the table next to him, and a cheroot was smoldering in the ashtray. No lights burned in the darkened cabin, but a splash of moonlight entered through the small window and fell across the bed. He was watching Greta sleep.

Nell Garvin's instincts had been right on target when she insinuated back in Memphis that either Faro had already bedded his young traveling companion or would eventually. It was odd, Faro thought, that she seemed to have recognized that inevitability even before he himself did. But why had he done it, he wondered.

One obvious reason, of course, was the physical release that sex provided. He had grown accustomed to that over the years. But it wasn't as if he would have gone crazy if he had tried to contain his horniness during a three-day boat trip down the Mississippi. He was hardly a slave to such things.

It had more to do, he thought, with the element of conquest. When there was a beautiful woman around, a force inside him usually compelled him to try for her. Often, though, he had to admit that it wasn't worth the effort and the complications which usually arose. In the heat of passion earlier this evening, Greta had mumbled some endearments to him which were decidedly unsettling. All he had been concentrating on was the screwing. The next thing he knew, she would be fishing for reassurances concerning his lasting affection and fidelity, and the good times would certainly come to an end the second he explained to her where they really stood.

The journey was more than half over now. They had stopped briefly in Vicksburg late the previous afternoon to take on cargo and passengers, and now they were steaming on down the river right on schedule. Barring accidents or unexpected delays, they would reach New Orleans the day after tomorrow. Things would work out, he assured himself. He would deliver Greta safely to Winchell in a few more days, and then they would have their fortune and their future together to enjoy. And surely the banker would be delighted with the new and exciting woman that Faro turned over to him.

When Greta rolled over to the center of the bed and spread her body comfortably across it, Faro decided not to try to rejoin her. The heat and the narrowness of these steamboat beds didn't make for good sleeping in pairs, and he knew he would rest better back in his own cabin. He reached for his clothes and began dressing. As Faro eased the cabin door open to leave, he glanced back a final time at the young woman. She was still deeply asleep.

Faro tensed as something hard jammed against his ribs and a man behind him ordered, "Freeze, asshole." Though the man spoke in a hushed tone, Faro immediately recognized Turk Bishop's voice.

"Now turn real slow and don't give me no reason to splatter your guts all over this deck here," the private detective told him. Faro complied with the instructions, raising his hands to shoulder height and turning cautiously.

It was apparent that Bishop did not intend for tonight to be a repeat of the scene between them on the train. He had brought help along this time. Two men stood slightly behind him in the shadows, and both of them were armed with revolvers just as the detective was.

Faro knew what serious trouble he was in as soon as he saw Bishop's battered condition. His head looked like something a grizzly bear had chewed up and then spit out. His left arm was in a sling across his chest, and when he moved slightly on the deck, he limped noticeably. The twisted expression of anger on his face indicated that he was none too happy with the man who was responsible for the shape he was in now.

"Did you really think you could shake me off your tail so easy, asshole?" Bishop snarled. "Get back inside there before somebody spots us out here with these guns."

With three pistols pointed at his belly, Faro had no choice but to obey. Awakened by the unexpected commotion of four grown men crowding into her cabin, Greta sat bolt upright in the bed. She started to protest, but one of Bishop's men pounced on her immediately, subduing her with one arm around her body and the other hand across her mouth. She struggled uselessly for a moment, then lay still, staring up at her captor with terrified cow eyes. The detective's other assistant closed the door, then stood with his back to it, out of the way.

"Before you do whatever you've got in mind to do to me," Faro said, "I'd sure like to know how you located us."

"It wasn't as hard as you might imagine," Bishop told him, obviously proud of his detective work. "A little cash spread around in the right places goes a long way in a situation like this. First I found out from a ticket agent at the train station that two people fitting your descriptions had cashed in the second halves of their tickets to New Orleans. That meant that you didn't intend to travel on by train, but I guessed that you were probably still headed in the same direction. I checked around and found out that the *Sweet Beaulah* had just left heading south, and a clerk in the steamboat line's office said he had sold two tickets to a man fitting your description. He also provided me with a name to fit the face."

"And from there you caught a train to Vicksburg," Faro suggested, "knowing you could still get there before the steamboat did."

"Exactly," Bishop said. His grin was twisted and grotesque. "In Natchez I hired my two associates here as insurance, then purchased tickets for the three of us on the *Beaulah*. And here we are."

"Damned smart of you, Bishop," Faro commented. "Mr. Sylvester back at the good old Fidelity Trust should give you an extra pat on the head for that piece of work when you return the, uh, merchandise to him."

"Don't try to bullshit me, Blake," the detective said. "You know damn good and well that's not what

I've got in mind. But before we get through, the two of you will probably be wishing that we'd just turned you over to the law." He glanced toward Greta, and for a moment his eyes remained on her, taking in the features of her naked body. The man who was holding her had swallowed one of her breasts in his hand and was harshly fondling it.

"If she'll promise not to scream, I guess you can let her go, Newt," the detective said.

"How about it, little lady?" Newt asked, abusing her breast even more cruelly. "You think you can keep your yap shut if I take my hand away?" Greta nodded that she could. As soon as she was released, she tried to pull the bedsheet up to cover her nakedness, but Newt wouldn't permit it. He was enjoying what he saw too much to allow her to hide it. Across the room, the second man was staring at Greta with equal appetite.

"First things first, boys," Bishop told his men. Then, turning to Faro, he said, "All right, Blake. Where's the money?"

"I don't know," Faro said. He honestly didn't, though he knew there was an excellent chance that Greta had hidden it somewhere in this cabin. What else could she have done with it?

The detective raised his pistol almost casually and crashed it against the side of Faro's head, staggering him back a couple of steps. "This is stupid, Blake," he complained. "I know you wouldn't have left it in Memphis, so you're bound to have it here on the boat with you. Now I do intend to have a piece of your hide before I leave as payback for throwing me off that fucking train, but the whole thing doesn't have to get too awful gruesome unless you force my hand."

"Goddamnit, I don't know where the money is!" Faro insisted.

"Then how about you, little lady?" Bishop said, turning to Greta. "Would you rather talk to me now, or let Newt make a believer out of you first?"

Greta was crying and trembling with fear, trying without much success to conceal the exposed parts of her body with her hands and arms. "Please . . . !" she whimpered weakly.

"Newt . . ." Bishop said.

Newt grabbed Greta by the hair, yanking her head back painfully, then drew a long sheath knife from his belt and waved it in front of her face. Faro tried to interfere, but Bishop kept him pinned against the wall with the barrel of his pistol lodged against his throat.

As Faro watched in horror, Newt lowered the blade of his knife until it hovered between her breasts. He touched it lightly against her and made a hairline cut in her skin about two inches long. Greta seemed mesmerized by the lethal blade and by the blood it had drawn from her flesh.

"For Chrissake, tell them where the goddamn money is!" Faro exclaimed. *"Can't you see the bastard would love to slice you to pieces!"*

"It's . . ." she began hesitantly. "It's . . ." Her arm raised and she pointed toward the small closet of her cabin. "In the black leather case," she said.

"Cover this guy for me, Bob," Bishop told the man at the door. Then he opened the closet and began rummaging around through Greta's personal belongings until he found the small leather case containing the money. He pulled it out and opened it briefly to confirm that it was the genuine article, then turned to his men with a broad grin of triumph.

"By God, this is it!" he exclaimed. "And don't worry, boys. Both of you will get those bonuses I promised you."

"I want to start getting my bonus right now. I want me some of this." Newt grinned, brandishing Greta by the grip he still had on her hair. He tossed her carelessly back on her bed, then stood up and began opening his trousers.

"I might have to try some of that twitch myself," Bob commented as he watched his companion's preparations. "Long as we got it right here handy."

"A'right, but hurry up with it!" Bishop told them. "And keep your hand over her mouth so's she won't holler while you're fucking her."

Lying flat on her back on the bed, Greta seemed practically comatose as she watched Newt drop his pants and crawl astraddle of her on the bed. Her eyes were dull and lusterless, and she offered no resistance as her attacker clamped his hand across her mouth and sprawled his body atop hers. Faro watched with growing rage as Newt hunched around on her, trying clumsily to make his insertion, but Bishop wasn't allowing him the slightest opportunity to interfere.

When Newt finally gained entry, Greta winced with pain and a spark of anger came alive in her eyes. She struggled as the big man shoved more deeply into her, and she arched her head back. Without warning, Newt roared out in pain as Greta's teeth clamped onto the fleshy part of his hand.

"You're gonna wake the whole goddamn boat!" Bishop hissed angrily.

"The bitch bit me!" Newt snarled. He raised up onto one elbow and drew back his injured hand to strike her, but Greta didn't give him the chance. She snaked her hand down between their bodies, grabbed his testicles and gave them a sharp twist. Newt bellowed out again in agony. During the instant that he was immobilized by the pain, Greta shoved against his chest and tumbled him sideways off the bed.

The second of confusion which followed provided Faro with his opportunity to act. When he saw the barrel of Bishop's revolver waver and swing slightly to the side, he took hold of the weapon and gave the detective a hard shove backward. Bob had been standing directly behind his employer, and his gun went off the instant that Bishop crashed into him. Faro felt the detective's hand go slack on the revolver and snatched it out of his grasp.

Down on the floor, Newt had more problems than he could handle. With one hand he was trying to retrieve a weapon from the tangle of clothes around his ankles, while he attempted to ward off a furious attack from Greta with the other. She had one hand locked onto his hair, just as he had been holding her moments before, while she raked at his face and eyes with the fingernails of the other.

As Bishop's body sagged to the floor, landing in a heap atop Newt, Faro raised his confiscated revolver and fired it point blank at Bob's chest. Bob had been trying to do exactly the same thing, but he was a fraction of a second too slow. His head dropped and his eyes stared in disbelief at the bloody hole in the middle of his body. Then he tumbled forward on top of Bishop.

With an insane roar, Newt wrestled free from the weight of his dead companions and tried to get up. He caught Greta across her chest with a backhand blow which hurled her against the cabin wall, then slashed at Faro with the knife that he had somehow managed to retrieve from its sheath. The tip of the razor-sharp blade sliced Faro's trousers, barely grazing the flesh of his leg before he could leap back out of reach.

"Drop that goddamn knife!" Faro commanded, brandishing the pistol.

"Fuck you!" Newt snarled. He pulled one leg free and braced it against the bed to make a lunge.

Faro raised the barrel of the revolver until it was pointing at the center of the man's face and pulled the trigger.

"Holy Moses an' the chillun of Israel!" the black steward exclaimed from the open doorway of Greta's cabin. He had arrived outside the door only seconds after the last shot was fired, but it had taken Faro a moment to get the feet of one of the dead men out of the way so the door could be opened.

"They just busted in here out of nowhere and attacked us!" Faro explained. "I don't even know who they are!"

The steward didn't say anything. His eyes were riveted on the clutter of dead bodies on the floor. Faro glanced over to where Greta sat naked on the bed, stunned and unmoving. He scrambled over to her and pulled the sheet up around her to cover her body. She hardly seemed to notice.

"Go get somebody, for heaven's sake," Faro snapped at the steward. "Get the captain or somebody."

A crowd had already started to gather behind the steward, and he tried ineffectively to push through them, but it proved to be unnecessary. Soon the captain of the *Sweet Beaulah* came shoving through the throng of people.

Captain Yarborough was scowling mightily as he stopped in the doorway and surveyed the scene.

When his gaze swept in Faro's direction, Faro realized he was still holding the revolver he had used to kill two of the men. He quickly dropped it to the floor.

"They broke in here and attacked us!" Faro told the captain. "I don't know why, and I don't know who they are."

The captain glanced over to Greta and he asked, "What about her? What happened to her?"

"I think we need to discuss this in private," Faro said, suddenly aware of the dozen or so sets of ears hovering on the walkway outside the door. "If you'll let me take the young lady down to my cabin and give her a moment to get some clothes on, we can tell you everything that happened. Is that all right?"

While Faro was gathering up some clothes for Greta, he shoved the briefcase of money under some things in the closet as inconspicuously as possible. The crowd parted before them as he led Greta, still wrapped in the sheet, down the walkway to his room. He unlocked his door and entered alone with her. She seemed to be recovering slightly from the shock of what had happened.

"Put these things on while we talk," Faro told her, pitching the bundle of clothing on the bed. "In a minute the captain is going to be asking us all kinds of questions about what happened down there, and our stories are going to have to match pretty closely to be believable. Of course we can't mention the money, so I guess the only other motive we can give them is rape."

"This is all going to be so ugly, Faro," Greta complained. "How can I tell a total stranger like the captain what that man did to me?"

"If you seem upset enough, he'll probably let me do all the talking," Faro suggested. "When he comes in, you just sit there sniffling and hiding your face. I'll handle the rest."

As soon as Greta was dressed, Faro invited the captain in and began to tell him what he could about the killings. Greta played her part well, sitting on the far end of the bed, apparently so ashamed and upset that she was unable to raise her face from her damp hankie.

Faro explained that the young lady had been feeling nauseated earlier in the evening and that he had stopped by her cabin to make sure she was all right. They had visited for a few minutes, then as he was leaving he encountered the three men on the walkway outside. One of them happened to see Greta through the open door, and they forced their way into the cabin, taking Faro with them. While holding Faro at gunpoint, they made her strip down and prepared to have their way with her. But Greta rebelled. From there on, Faro was able to relate the details exactly as they happened.

"I must commend both of you for your bravery," the captain said when Faro was finished, "and I offer my sincere apologies that this incident took place on my boat. But I have to admit that it all strikes me as very strange."

"It was more than strange," Faro agreed. "It was downright crazy!"

"Those three men had just boarded the *Beaulah* a few hours before. I can't see that they would have come on board just on the chance of stumbling across this sort of opportunity, and it seems stupid for them to believe they could commit such a crime and get away with it."

"Nobody said they were intelligent," Faro said, his tone slightly guarded. "Somehow, Captain Yarborough, I'm getting the feeling that you suspect I'm lying to you."

"Not necessarily," the captain replied. "I'm just saying that a lot of this doesn't make any sense to me."

"Nonetheless, sir . . ." Faro replied haughtily.

The captain looked over toward Greta, who was still whimpering on her corner of the bed. "Perhaps we've talked enough about this for the time being," he said. "I'm sure the young lady is very upset and needs a good rest. I'll arrange with the steward to have her things moved to another cabin and to check on her from time to time."

"I can do that," Faro said. "I'll take care of her."

"Well, Mr. Blake," the captain began hesitantly, "I'm afraid that might be difficult."

"And why's that?"

"Because I'm going to have to request that you remain in your cabin until we reach our next stop, which will be Baton Rouge. It's really only a formality, I assure you, but you are responsible for three deaths on board my boat. It is a matter for the authorities, and until I can turn you over to them, you must be confined."

"This is ridiculous!" Faro protested.

"Perhaps," Yarborough told him calmly. "But I am in charge of this vessel, and I must insist that you comply with my wishes. Guards will be posted outside your door, and the young lady will be taken care of in another location."

There seemed little Faro could do about the situation. The captain's mind was obviously made up. But in spite of everything, Faro knew he was still getting out easily. If the captain knew the whole truth about the money and everything else, Faro would probably have ended up in chains instead of simply being confined to his cabin. He was permitted another moment alone with Greta, during which he tried to offer her some reassurances, then the steward came to take her to her new cabin. As Faro opened his door to let her out, he saw that two armed crewmen had taken up positions on the walkway outside.

Chapter Twelve

Faro lay on his back on the bed, staring at the lamp, which burned at a dim glow on the wall by the door. He was coated with a clammy sweat which he knew was only partially caused by the muggy heat in the small compartment. He was thinking about death.

Every time he closed his eyes, his mind recalled the amazed expression of the man named Bob an instant after he was shot. Faro had seen that expression on the faces of men before, the stark, terrified look of a human being who suddenly realizes he is mortal and that his life is about to end.

Killing them had been necessary. Faro was certain of that, and he felt no particular guilt about being the one to end the lives of such men. But he had killed enough men before to know that there was an inevitable aftermath to such a deed. Sometimes it came in the form of shakes and sweats, and other times it manifested itself as a deep, burning resentment toward the dead man for forcing him to become a killer once again. A lot of times he found himself getting drunk or getting laid afterward, either of which served to drain away some of the emotional tension.

In retrospect, Faro was starting to realize how complicated this whole situation might become if the authorities in Baton Rouge did their job properly. Bishop most likely still had his identification card on him, and a couple of telegrams to St. Louis would probably reveal that he was supposed to be working for the bank. That inevitably would lead to the conclusion that he and Greta had stolen the money from the Fidelity Trust vault and killed the men sent to bring them to justice. Next would come more years in prison than Faro cared to consider.

Escape was the only solution, but he had yet to figure out how he could possibly get past his guards, locate Greta and get her and the money safely off the boat and onto dry land. His captors were an inefficient lot. They had taken his derringer, but they neglected to search his luggage for any other weapons. He still had the sawed-off shotgun which he always carried in his advantage tool case. Yet the idea of wandering around the boat, blasting everybody who got in his way until he and Greta could escape was repulsive. And it was dangerous.

He heard voices on the walkway outside his door. In a moment a key turned in the lock and the door swung open. Captain Yarborough came in a couple of steps, then closed the door behind him.

"Is everything all right, Mr. Blake?" Yarborough asked.

"Just dandy," Faro grumbled, not even bothering to rise from the bed.

"I have some news for you that I'm afraid you

won't like," the captain announced. "A short time ago my steward went to check on your friend, Grace Worthington, and he found her cabin empty. We've just completed a search of the entire boat, and she seems to be gone. A rowboat which was tied to the stern is also missing."

Faro tried to conceal the rush of alarm he felt. Greta must have come to the same general conclusions he had about what awaited them in Baton Rouge and decided to take independent action to keep herself out of trouble.

"I believed there was no need to have her guarded, but apparently I was mistaken," Yarborough commented.

"Apparently," Faro said. "So what are you going to do about it?"

"There's not much I can do except report it to the authorities along with everything else. It would be senseless to turn around and search for her in this darkness, and if she's been gone any length of time, she's probably reached the bank by now anyway. We're only running about three hundred feet out."

"Damnit all anyway!" Faro complained bitterly. "You know what this means, don't you? She was the only witness to what happened down in her cabin. She's the only one who could have confirmed that I was justified in what I did. And now with her gone . . ."

"The situation would seem to speak for itself," the captain pointed out. "Judging by the circumstances, it hardly seems likely that you lured those three men in there just so you could kill them with their own weapons. I still think that your visit with the authorities will be a simple formality."

Sure, a long-term formality, Faro thought bitterly. *About twenty years worth!*

"At any rate," Yarborough continued, "we'll find out in another few hours. We're scheduled to reach Baton Rouge about dawn."

"Don't forget to wake me," Faro grumbled. "I'd hate to miss all the fun."

He laid his plans carefully, knowing he would have only one chance to get it right. His first step was to take everything he would need from his suitcase, including his shaving gear and a few other personal articles, and put them in his advantage case along with his gambling tools. Before closing the case, he took the sawed-off shotgun out and loaded it. Next he stripped down to his cotton drawers and neatly stacked his clothes and boots atop the case. And finally he removed two of the wooden shelves from the closet, sandwiched his case and clothing between them and tied the whole thing into a neat bundle with strips torn from his bed sheet.

The waiting was the most difficult part. All through the night, the two guards outside his door had wandered off, one at a time, presumably for food, water or at nature's urging. But now that all his preparations were made, the pair had parked themselves like stones before the door. The minutes dragged by with tedious slowness as he hovered near the window, waiting for one of them to leave.

At least half an hour passed before one of the men stood up from his chair and told his companion, "My belly's starting to growl. I think I'll see if the cook's got any leftovers down in the galley."

"Bring me some coffee on your way back," the other man told him.

Faro moved to the door and paused, giving the first man time to get to the end of the walkway and around a corner. Then he eased the door open.

When the lone guard glanced around, he found himself staring at the twin barrels of Faro's shotgun.

"I'm getting lonely in here," Faro told the guard. "Why don't you step in and pay me a little visit."

The guard glanced down at Faro's state of undress, then looked back at his face with an expression of utter revulsion. "Nothin' doin', you sick son of a bitch!" he said.

"Goddamn!" Faro growled, jamming the shotgun against the guard's chest. "I ain't going to jump on your bones, you jackass! Can't you see I'm planning to escape?"

The guard actually seemed relieved by the explanation and rose from his chair without further protest. Once he was inside the cabin, Faro made him stand beside the bed, then rapped him across the back of the skull with the butt of his shotgun. He fell in a neat heap on top of the mattress, and Faro rifled his pockets until he located his Reid's derringer.

Faro picked up his bundle of belongings and dashed out of the cabin, carrying the shotgun in his right hand like a pistol. When he reached the rear of the boat, he lodged the gun down under the torn strips of sheet and stepped over the railing with his burden in hand. He prayed that it would float, because he knew he would need the buoyance in the treacherous Mississippi currents.

Back behind him from the direction of his cabin he heard a voice call out loudly, "Hey you! Hold it right there!" Faro didn't even pause to glance back. Holding his bundle tightly in his arms, he shoved off with his legs and plunged down into the churning, murky depths of the great river.

Faro's arms felt as if they were about to be ripped

from their sockets, and the palms of his hands were so blistered and raw that he wouldn't be able to do justice to a deck of cards for a month. But still he kept rowing. He had been propelling the small john boat against the current on the eastern side of the Mississippi since dawn. Now, sometime past noon, he believed he might finally be nearing the vicinity where Greta had abandoned him and made for the bank. Every pull against the oars and every pain that lanced through his hands and arms only served to increase the seething fury inside him.

After what had seemed like hours in the water, swimming against the heavy currents and the insistent undertow of the river, Faro had finally reached the bank a couple of hours before dawn. His body just barely had enough strength left in it to drag his burden up a steep bank of crumbling mud before he collapsed into exhausted sleep.

The sun had just started to rise when an old man in a tiny boat hailed him from the edge of the water. Faro raised up and looked down at him, relieving the old man's fears that he might be dead. Within a few minutes Faro had negotiated to buy the boat for little more than five times what it was worth.

Faro figured it might take him days to tromp northward along the riverbank, snaking his way through the thick brush and skirting the wide flooded areas which were bound to lie in his path. And by the time he did manage to pick up the thread of Greta's trail, if he was ever that fortunate, she would be long gone. But he could make the trip in just a few hours by boat, and the chances were much greater that he could catch up with her. It was a gamble, of course. There was no guarantee that she even made for the Mississippi side of the river instead of going to the Louisiana side. But that bank had been much closer when she made her escape, and Faro was, after all, in the business of taking calculated risks.

If he hadn't been watching the bank so closely, he might have passed right on by the rowboat without ever noticing it. It was hidden about twenty feet up in a small inlet, covered over with fresh brush. As he rowed closer, Faro rejoiced when he saw the steamboat's name painted across the back bulkhead of the abandoned craft. There was no doubt that this was where Greta had landed.

Several things about the scene confused Faro, however. One thing was the heavy brush which nearly concealed the boat. Greta would have had neither the tools nor the desire to do such a thing. Escape was all she would have been thinking about. And in addition, several long sets of furrowed footprints led up the steep, ten-foot slope to the bank above. That didn't make any sense either. Faro decided it was time for caution until he learned a little more about what was going on.

The first thing he did was point his boat back into the river and row back south for about a quarter of a mile. When he found a shallow creek which seemed suitable to his purposes, he threw his belongings up onto the bank, piled a few heavy stones into his boat and then tipped it to the side until it sank. It was scarcely visible lying on the bottom of the creek, and he knew that as small as it was he would be able to raise it again if the need arose. Then he started back north toward where Greta's boat was hidden.

After fifteen minutes spent examining the area, Faro wasn't any closer to understanding what had gone on here than he had been to start with. All he knew was that the boat was here and Greta wasn't. Three or four sets of tracks led away from the scene in a northeasterly direction, but they disappeared as soon as he entered a nearby patch of woods.

Before resuming the pursuit, Faro dropped down tiredly on the creek bank to rest. A few dozen feet up the creek was a small lovely pool. Its clear, dark water contrasted strikingly with the flat brown shade of the Mississippi itself, and after a moment Faro decided that the pool was too inviting to resist. He walked up to its edge, stripped off his clothes and fell in. He found a shallow, mossy spot next to the bank and just lay there for a while, letting the cool, rippling water soothe his aching shoulders and exhausted body. He almost let sleep claim him, but caught himself just before he drifted off. There was too much to do, he decided, sitting up abruptly in the water. As close as he probably was to Greta at this moment, it would be crazy to waste another minute here, even on such a delicious luxury as sleep. With a determined groan, he stood up and started toward his clothes.

"Mercy me! Will you lookit what's washed up out of the river now." The young woman who made the statement was sitting on the ground beside Faro's clothing, examining him from head to foot with unabashed delight. Her presence there was startling enough in itself, but what bothered Faro even more than her unexpected appearance was the shotgun which she held in her hands. It was his gun!

"My, my, my!" She grinned, standing up and starting toward where he stood. Faro held his ground, trying to act calmer than he felt. "When you was sprawled out over yonder in the crick, I judged you for a fine hunk of manhood," she told him. "An' I shore was right."

Faro judged her to be about twenty, and not bad-looking either for a corn-fed hill woman. She wore a long skirt that dragged the ground behind her as she walked, and a threadbare cotton blouse which still bore the fading imprints of the flour sacks from which it was made. Her long black hair hung in a tangle around her tanned face, and one of her front teeth was missing on the top left side. She had quite a pretty face, though her smile was slightly discomforting and some sort of menace shone just beneath the surface of her lustrous dark eyes.

Holding the shotgun with unsettling familiarity, she reached out and lifted Faro's penis with its cool twin barrels. "Uh huh," she noted. "I judged this here thang about right, too. I had me a feelin' soon's I come out of the woods an' spotted you."

"Just be careful with that scattergun, miss," Faro cautioned her. "I hadn't really got all the use out of that 'thang' that I intend to."

The woman laughed out loud at that. "I bet you hadn't, big fellow." She grinned. "But I'll bet you've got some use out of it anyways." She lowered the barrel of the gun, letting his grateful personals return to their normal position. Then she turned her back to him and went back over to sit down beside his pile of clothes. From her casual attitude, Faro wasn't sure whether he was supposed to be her captive or not. He decided to remain cautious until she gave him some indication one way or the other.

"My name is Faro Blake," he offered at last. "What's yours?"

"It's Dawn," she replied. "Really it's Ruta Dawn Fernshaw, but I'm partial to usin' my middle name."

"It's a pretty name," Faro said. "Can I call you Dawn?"

"I don't see no harm in it. Seems like we've done started ourselves out on a pretty personal basis already." She smiled. As she spoke, her eyes scanned his body with undeniable appetite. Faro might have appreciated the looks more if she put the gun aside.

"Would you mind if I put my clothes on, Dawn?" he asked.

"Why? You chilly?"

"No."

"Then why?"

"I thought it might put you more at ease if I was dressed," he suggested.

"Not really," Dawn said with a smile. "I like you fine thisaway. Why don't you sit yourself down an' let's talk. Maybe you'd like to tell me what in blazes you're doin' way out here in the middle of nowhere."

Faro settled on the soft grass a few feet away from her, and he began to feel a little better when she laid the shotgun on the ground beside her leg. "You're going to find this a little hard to believe," he said, "but I jumped off a steamboat and swam ashore."

"That does sound like an addlebrained thang to do," she judged.

"Well, I had some trouble with some fellows, and the captain of the boat decided he was going to turn me over to the law down in Baton Rouge. But I've never been particularly fond of messing with the law when I could find a way around it, so I gathered up some things and I jumped. It's as simple as that." Faro paused a moment, then said, "Now it's your turn, Dawn. What are you doing out here?"

"This here's my daddy's land, so it ain't nothin' unusual atall for me to be here. But the fact is, I come down today to check on that boat in the bushes up yonder. You know, it's a downright curious thang. Last night my brothers was out this way coon huntin' an' they found theirselves a woman. Then today they send me down here to check on her boat, an' lo an' behold if I don't find myself a man in the exact same spot!" She smiled broadly at him and gave him a knowing wink. "Maybe daddy'll let me do with you what my brother Little Bob figgers on doin' with that woman of his!"

"He found a woman, huh?" Faro said, trying to show only casual curiosity.

"A looker, she is," Dawn said. "Daddy Jonah says she looks like a fancy-house hoor, but Little Bob's right taken with her. Says he aims to marry up with her soon's he can break her spirit some. She ain't your woman is she?"

"I don't have a woman," Faro told her.

"Good," Dawn said. "I like that jes' fine."

The young hillbilly woman seemed eager to put her new discovery to some practical use, but she couldn't figure out a way to do that and still keep the gun trained on him. Finally she allowed him to get dressed, explaining that she was taking him off to meet "Daddy Jonah."

"But don't you go fergittin' who catched you fair an' square," Dawn said as they started away from the river, "an' who has dibs on you."

They made their way through about a half mile of woods, skirting occasional dense pine thickets and low-lying marshy areas. The forest was crisscrossed with a number of footpaths, most of which appeared to receive regular use. Before long Faro had a pretty good idea concerning the uses to which the Fernshaws probably put this wooded area. The air around them was filled with the unmistakable odor of sour mash cooking over a charcoal fire, but he thought it best not to mention the subject to Dawn. Moonshiners usually became touchy when strangers showed any interest in their business.

Eventually they emerged into a flat clearing about half an acre in size. A dilapidated frame house quite unlike any structure Faro had ever seen sat in the center of the clearing. Once upon a time it had probably been a typical "dogtrot" house, with one large room on either side, and an open breezeway, or dogtrot, down the middle. But someone with a talent for slipshod carpentry had added a number of extra rooms to the sides and rear of the original building. Now it was a disaster of oddly clashing roof lines, ill-fitting plank walls and tilting brick chimneys.

Vegetables and weeds thrived in a large garden plot directly behind the house. Beyond the garden were a couple of ruined sheds and a large barn which looked ready to collapse before the first stout breeze which assaulted it. A few mangy cows and a pair of pissed-off looking plow mules stood ankle-deep in manure in the barnyard.

But for all its disrepair and neglect, there was obviously one commodity which was produced in abundance on this farmstead. As soon as Faro and Dawn appeared at the edge of the clearing, youngsters of all ages began to pour out of the doors and windows of the house and come howling in their direction. They beseiged Faro immediately, examining him as if he might be some alien creature, plucking at his clothes with grimy fingers, grabbing for the advantage tool case which he held, and plunging their hands down into his pockets to pilfer anything he could not protect. It took Dawn a moment to bring this swarming rabble under control and to herd them off to a more secure distance.

"My God," Faro grumbled to Dawn. "What are you running here anyway? Some kind of breeding farm for yard rats?" At least fifteen filthy children from infancy to early teens surrounded them.

"These here is my brothers an' sisters," Dawn explained. "Daddy Jonah's done wore out my mama an' one other wife makin' young-uns, an' las' fall he married number three. She's even younger'n me, jes' nineteen, but she's already knocked up."

"Sounds like a man that likes his lovin'," Faro commented.

"An' don't get 'round to much else," Dawn confirmed. "Now that Little Bob and a couple of the other boys is old enough to tend the fambly business, Daddy jes' lays around the place most of the time, waitin' for his tallywhacker to swell up so's he can get back to doin' what he does best."

A man stepped into view as they neared the crumbling front porch of the house, and Faro realized that he must be the single-minded patriarch of this motley clan, "Daddy" Jonah Fernshaw. He was a tall man with a hogshead chest and a huge belly which spilled across the front of his pants like a hundredweight sack of flour about to fall off a shelf. His thick black hair clung in wiry confusion to the top of his head, and his matted beard was streaked with wide bands of steel gray. There was an innate look of menace in his eyes, and when he glanced at Faro, he looked like he would rather kill him than bother listening to why he was there. But Dawn wasn't about to let that happen.

"Looka here, Daddy!" she announced proudly. "I found me a feller down by the river."

"What in the hell you talking about, girl?" her father growled angrily. One of his gnarled paws rose to claw at a reeking armpit, then dropped down to give his crotch an affectionate squeeze.

"He fell off a riverboat an' I brung him in," Dawn explained. "Kin I keep him, Daddy? Like Little Bob done with that fancy of his?"

"Cain't keep no man like you does a woman," Fernshaw explained irritably.

"Oh, I know that," Dawn said. "But I could keep 'im for a spell anyways. I been needin' me some man attention somethin' awful!"

The old man seemed to respond to that argument, but he still found the suggestion objectionable. "Probably a gawddamn lawman, or worse," he said.

Faro had to wonder what could be worse under these circumstances.

"Is that what you be, mister?" Fernshaw asked.

"Absolutely not," Faro told him. "As a matter of fact, I'm not getting on too well with the law myself right now." He was beginning to get some bad feelings about this whole situation, and he thought it best to go along with these maniacs for the time being. "This girl of yours strikes me as a fine-looking little heifer, and I can't say it would bother me too much to give her what she needs."

"See there, Daddy!" Dawn announced brightly. "He ain't no law, an' he won't be a bit of bother."

"A'right, you kin keep 'im down to the barn fer the time bein'," the old man conceded at last. "But if he gits loose an' stirs up any trouble, it's your ass, Myra Jean."

"I'm Ruta Dawn, Daddy," Dawn told him patiently. "Myra Jean's the next younger than me."

"Don't backsass me, girl," Fernshaw warned as he turned back to the house. "How do you 'spect me to keep up with all your gawddamn names?"

Chapter Thirteen

Turnip greens and cornbread weren't the most sumptuous fare Faro had ever tasted, but considering the fact that it had been nearly twenty-four hours since he had last eaten, they tasted pretty good going down and calmed the gnawing in his stomach quite satisfactorily. He wasn't any too happy about the gallery of grimy youngsters who flanked him on three sides as he ate, either, but he realized that they meant no harm. They were just curious, gawking and pointing like a crowd of bumpkins just getting their first glimpse of the circus freak. The heavy manacle and chain which bound him to the center support post of the barn only served to make him that much more of an oddity.

Faro figured the chains and things must have been left over from the days when slaves were kept imprisoned in the barn at night. After securing him there early in the afternoon, Dawn had left him alone for the rest of the day as she went about her routine farm work. But the situation wasn't that uncomfortable. The barn was airy and cool, and he had a soft bed of fresh hay to lie on. He had spent most of the afternoon catching up on his sleep. At dusk, one of the girls brought him his supper, and the rest of the brood tagged along to ogle their sister's prize.

Faro didn't spend much time worrying about his situation. The Reid's derringer was still nestled comfortably in the small pocket inside his jacket, ready to purchase his freedom for him any time he wanted it. In addition, he had discovered just a few minutes after Dawn chained him up how easy it was to pick the antique lock on the manacle around his ankle. He had opened and closed it a few times for practice, then left it secured around his leg before he went to sleep. He wasn't ready to make his escape just yet. He had to remain a willing captive here until he learned more about where Greta was and how much trouble it would be to free her.

He figured the Fernshaws must be holding Greta prisoner somewhere in their house, but he doubted that they had any idea about the money. Dawn had made no mention of it when she was talking about her brother's new treasure, and it didn't seem likely that the clan would be going about their business as usual if they had suddenly come into such wealth.

So the first thing was to get Greta out of here, and the next was to make her tell him what she had done with the hundred thousand dollars.

The interior of the barn was dim by the time Faro finished his supper and set the plate aside. The children were growing accustomed to him and had started to get friendly.

"Whereat did you come from, mister?" one of the boys asked. He was a towheaded youth of about ten, obviously bolder than the rest.

"Out of the river," Faro replied.

"Before that I mean."

"From Memphis, and before that, from St. Louis."

"Our daddy was in Memphis once," the boy revealed proudly. "He said they got roads made out of bricks there, an' buildin's as tall as six houses piled up one on top of t'other. Is that so?"

"They're making them even taller than that," Faro said. "And a couple of them have electric lights in them now."

"'Letrit lights?" the youth asked. "What's that?"

"It's a kind of light that doesn't use any kerosene or oil. It runs off electricity that comes through a wire."

"You're joshin' us, now!" the boy scoffed. "They ain't no sucha thing!"

"Yeah, you're right, sonny." Faro chuckled. "I was just making up a story to see if you would swallow it."

A door at the front of the barn scraped open, and Dawn came in, carrying a lantern in one hand and Faro's shotgun in the other. She waded into the midst of Faro's audience and announced, "Some of you young-uns got after-dinner chores to do, an' it's bedtime for the rest. Now git! All of you!" Carping and complaining, the children began to file out of the barn, and when the last one was gone, Dawn closed and barred the door. Then she turned to Faro. She had changed into a clean dress, and her long dark hair glistened from a recent brushing. When she came closer, Faro detected the scent of lye soap and cheap toilet water.

"I sure hope you're gonna be nice," she said as she hung the lantern on a hook along one wall. "Daddy says if you ain't, he aims to cut you up an' feed you to his pack of huntin' dogs."

"In that case, I'll be on my best behavior," Faro announced with a smile.

"A'right, then. I'm gonna put this scattergun over by the door," she said. "But don't fergit. One holler from me an' the whole bunch of them will be on you like flies on cowpies. Daddy, an' Little Bob an' all the rest."

"You have my word," he assured her. Then as she put the gun aside, he added, "But I'm still not exactly clear on why you're keeping me here like this."

Walking back toward him with an intimate smile, she said throatily, "I think you know, a'right." Her fingers toyed with the top button of her dress, and in a moment it popped open, as if by accident. As she settled on the hay beside him, a second and a third button were opened, revealing an inviting expanse of soft cleavage.

"Daddy don't hardly never let me bring no beaus around," she explained quietly. "Says he don't want no strangers stickin' their noses in the fambly business. But I'm a growed-up woman now, an' there's times when a man could do me powerful good."

Faro grinned. "I think I get the message." He opened a couple more buttons down the front of her dress, then reached inside and caressed her breast through the fabric of her cotton undergarments. She sighed with pleasure and lay back contentedly on the hay.

"If you took a notion," she said, "I bet you could pleasure a gal somethin' wonderful."

"If I took a notion," Faro said. Suddenly he

deprived her of his touches. "But I have to admit that I'm none too fond of being chained to a post and having you demand such a thing of me."

"I told you about the dogs," she cautioned him.

"It would be a hell of a way for a man to have to go," Faro admitted, "just 'cause he couldn't get it up. But things would probably be a lot different if you were to make me *want* to do it."

She stared at him in confusion for a moment, then a smile of understanding slowly came to her face. "Mayhaps a peek at what I got to offer might help things along," she suggested.

"It sure couldn't hurt."

Dawn stood up and quickly removed her dress, then unbuttoned the front of her frayed cotton slip down to her waist. After that, she paused and asked, "You gonna make me get naked by myself?"

"I don't see much way for me to get my britches off over this chain," Faro said. "If you were to let me loose, I figure I'd be too wrapped up in what's going on here to think about running away."

"A'right," she conceded hesitantly, "but don't ferget . . ."

"I know. I could be dog meat."

After the young woman unchained him, Faro started to undress, spreading his clothes atop the hay to make a pallet for them. Dawn stood to one side watching him with a growing smile of anticipation. When he was nearly finished, she slid the straps of the slip off her shoulders and let it fall to the ground. Suddenly they stood face to face, both naked as newborns.

"Goodness gracious!" Dawn sighed. "A'ready I'm startin' to feel tingly all over!" Her eyes scanned down his body to his midsection, lingered there briefly, then rose back to his face. "An' it seems like you ain't a'gonna have no problem with this business neither."

"Seems like."

When he took her in his arms, her breasts pressed against his chest with surprising firmness. Her body was strong and supple from a lifetime of hard farm work, and her figure was ample and alluring. Grasping him around the waist with her arms, she tumbled back onto the hay and cut loose with a lusty laugh. "Come on, Mr. Fancy," she exclaimed. "We're both ready, so let's get to humping!"

Before Faro scarcely knew what was happening, she guided his erection to the proper spot and hoisted the sheath of her womanhood to accept it deep within her. She locked her legs around his hips and her arms around his back, clamped her teeth into the muscle of his shoulder and flew to hunching like some sort of crazed creature. Faro had never experienced anything quite like it. He felt, at the same time, both panic and an incredible surge of sexual stimulation.

Dawn's chesty moans, muted at first, became louder and louder as their frenzied copulation continued. Faro maintained no semblance of control. They rolled off his carefully constructed pallet, down off the pile of hay and across the hardpan floor, never breaking their primeval grip on one another the entire time. Faro eventually found himself on the bottom, with the slave chain grinding into his back as Dawn's lower body slammed almost painfully against his again and again.

When she began to come, her cries rose to an alarming volume. Thinking that at any moment the entire clan would rally at the barn to see what horrible things he was doing to her, Faro gave a hard shove with his arm, rolling her over onto her back.

As his hand clamped over her mouth to stifle her frantic wails, he pinned her body to the ground with his. Finally she bucked to a stop after her climax had run its delirious course and lay gasping for air. Faro guessed the whole thing had taken one minute or less.

"Goddamn, woman!" Faro exclaimed. He stared down at her in amazement as he withdrew and raised up off of her. Both their bodies were caked with sweat, hay and dirt, and Dawn's carefully brushed hair was now splayed in wild disarray around her head. Her eyes were closed and her mouth was wide open as she sucked in oxygen.

"That was *good!*" she told him breathlessly.

"I'll have to take your word for that," Faro grumbled. "It all happened so fast, I think I missed most of it."

"I was needful," Dawn said. "I didn't know how much so 'til I seen that thang of yours stand up an' say 'howdy.' After that, somethin' just went wild inside of me."

"Well I've never broke horses," he told her, "but I imagine it would have to be something like that. And now just look at us. I don't know which of us is the filthiest."

"We can fix that easy 'nough," she said. She slid out from under him and rose to her feet, then took his hand and led him toward a door at the rear of the barn. Out back they came to a six-foot wooden horse trough with a hand pump at one end. As Dawn moved to the pump, she told him, "Get in."

The water was as cold as December as it splashed across his bare back and shoulders, but in a minute Faro grew accustomed to it. Dawn pumped until the trough was overflowing, then came around and climbed in with him. They splashed and dunked one another like children, washing away the sweat and grime they had accumulated inside. When they were finished, Dawn's young body glistened in the moonlight like polished marble. Faro reached out and hefted her full breasts appreciatively, noting how the coldness had contracted her nipples to a delightful firmness. At the same time he felt her hands probing for his private parts under the water.

"I don't figger the stock would mind if we borried their trough for a spell," Dawn suggested.

"I'm not sure we can get ourselves situated in this damn thing, though," Faro said.

"Where there's a will, there's a way!"

Faro slid back in the trough until his head rested on the end, then Dawn raised herself carefully on top of him. It took them a minute to get their tangle of limbs arranged, but finally she was in position to slide her torso neatly down on top of his newly aroused erection. Her knees were pressing uncomfortably against his ribs and he realized how many splinters he was likely to accumulate in his backside before this whole thing was over, but the delightful sensations that her cool, moist cunt aroused in his stiff penis made it all worthwhile.

With surprising gentleness, Dawn raised herself up a few inches, then descended again, testing the fit and the feeling. It was just right. Her breasts, bobbing only inches from his face, suddenly seemed irresistible. As Faro leaned his head forward to engulf one delicious nipple in his mouth, Dawn's torso began to rise and fall above him with rhythmic precision.

Faro discovered that she was one hell of an orgasmic woman. Within a short time she had risen to another peak of excitement, but it arrived more calmly this time. He settled back in the water, letting her do the most work, and soon he felt his own climax welling up inside him. He closed his eyes and let it come, delighting in the flood of release that overwhelmed his body. But the mood was broken a minute later when he slid too low in the trough and gagged on the rush of water that invaded his mouth and nose. Laughing out loud, Dawn grabbed a handful of his hair and pulled his head back above the surface.

"Hold on there, Mr. Fancy." She giggled. "I ain't agonna let you get away from me that way, neither."

"It'd be a queer way to go." Faro chuckled. "Drowned whilst fucking a farm girl in a horse trough."

"And quite a waste, too," Dawn added.

Soon the position they were in became uncomfortable to Faro and he encouraged her to get off of him. They returned to the inside of the barn, where Faro flopped down tiredly on his clothes atop the hay. He laid his head back and closed his eyes, savoring the moment of after-sex euphoria.

"Girl, you sure know how to put it on a man," Faro mumbled contentedly. "I swear, whatever local hayseed you eventually marry up with is sure going to . . ." He sat up in surprise as he opened his eyes and looked over at Dawn. She was standing by the door with the sawed-off shotgun in her hands, pointing it at him once more. "What the hell?" he asked irritably.

"I figger I've had me enough for one night," she explained. "I sure hate to do this, but if I want you around tomorrow an' the day after that fer more of the same, seems like there ain't no other way."

Faro knew what she meant. He pulled on his

underclothes and trousers, then reached tiredly for the shackle and closed it around his ankle.

He gave Dawn a couple of hours to get back to the house and get settled in for the night. It was important that she didn't discover how easily he could free himself from his bondage, and he wanted to make sure the whole household was asleep before he ventured out of the barn. Finally when he thought it was safe, he picked the lock which held the shackle closed around his ankle and crept to the front door. No lights shone in any of the farmhouse windows.

Carrying his advantage tool case, which Dawn had stashed in a corner of the barn, he made his way cautiously to the house. He moved from one open window to another outside the house, peering inside each one and trying to make out whatever details he could. Several of the rooms were cluttered with sleeping children, piled four abreast on the beds and littering the floors on pallets. A loud chesty snoring rumbled out from another room, which led Faro to assume that was where Jonah Fernshaw must be sleeping. Finally he came to a room which contained only one bed with two sleeping mounds in it. He couldn't make out anything about the people, and he realized there was only one way to determine whether or not one of them was Greta.

Making as little sound as possible, Faro set a wooden box against the wall outside the window and stepped up on it. He had one leg through the opening and was about to put his weight down on it when his foot encountered something lumpy and alive. He heard an angry growl directly in front of him, and a set of sharp teeth clamped down hard on his leg.

Howling in unexpected pain, Faro shook his leg,

desperate to free himself from the fangs of the furious mongrel which was attacking him. He lost his balance and tumbled clumsily into the room, and in an instant the dog was on top of him, going for his throat. They tumbled around in confusion for a moment, but finally Faro gave a mighty heave and hurled the angry dog out the window. He heard the animal strike the ground outside and scamper yipping away into the night.

"What the fuck is going on?" somebody growled from the bed. A match flared in the darkness.

Faro was hurting in half a dozen places from the dog bites, but he knew he had to act fast to save himself. Reaching for the Reid's as he scrambled to his feet, he arrived at the foot of the bed just as the match ignited the wick of a lamp on a small table. A young man was sitting up on the bed, staring at him angrily, and beside him Greta Wimbley peeked out in terror from beneath the bedsheet. Faro brought the derringer to bear, ensuring that the man didn't reach for the rifle which leaned against the wall nearby.

"Faro!" Greta exclaimed. She sat bolt upright in the bed, revealing her naked condition. Her left arm was bound to the right arm of the man beside her by a short length of rope. "You've come to save me!"

That was the general idea, but things were not working out the way he had planned. An instant later he heard heavy footsteps in another part of the house and a door slammed open behind him. Jonah Fernshaw burst into the room, wearing a grimy suit of ragged long johns and carrying an enormous rifle in his hands. Behind him were two younger men, both armed and alert.

Faro didn't like the odds. At these close quarters, he stood a good chance of getting the old man and maybe even one of the others, but with so many weapons opposing him, he knew the chances were slim that he would survive the entire gunfight. He lowered the barrel of the Reid's as a sign of capitulation, then pitched the tiny weapon over on the bed.

"What in the goddamn hell are you doing in here?" the old man demanded, advancing on him menacingly.

"I came to get her," Faro explained. There was no use denying it.

"I thought you didn't know her," Jonah Fernshaw said. "An' even iffen you do, you ain't gettin' her. She's Little Bob's woman now."

"Me'n her is marryin' up," Little Bob confirmed from the bed.

"Faro, for God's sake, do something!" Greta squeaked from the bed. "It's been a nightmare here. You've got to help me!"

When Faro turned his head to look at her, he could see the misery clearly written on her features. There was a large blue bruise on her right shoulder, and another smaller one on the point of her jaw. Apparently Little Bob was none too gentle with his courtship rituals.

"I knowed it was a damn fool notion to keep your ass around here," Jonah Fernshaw told Faro. "But I allus was one to spile my young-uns. But the fun's over now."

"We fixin' to kill 'im, Daddy Jonah?" one of the young men asked gleefully from the doorway.

"Seems we hafta now," the old man answered.

"Lemme do it, Daddy," Little Bob begged.

"That wouldn't hardly be fittin' son, seein' as how you already been a'humpin his woman an' is fixin' to marry up with her soon's he's dead. I think the Holy

Book has somethin' to say agin them kinds of goin's on. I reckon the duty falls to me."

Stunned by the conversation, Greta tried to leap from the bed to Faro, but Little Bob yanked her back brutally by the rope which held them bound together. Faro had been taking it all in with amazement, and it seemed useless to offer any arguments in his defense. The decision of the one-man jury—Jonah Fernshaw—was already in. But a spark of an idea was beginning to ignite in Faro's brain.

"If your mind's made up, I guess I have no choice in the matter," he told the old man with calm resignation. "But despite everything, I still feel it's my Christian duty to warn you before you send me on to my great reward."

"Huh?" Fernshaw said. "What in blazes are you talkin' about?"

Faro glanced nervously around the room, letting his gaze linger on Greta. Then he replied, "We really should talk about this in private, just the two of us. It will only take a minute, and then you can do what you must."

Jonah Fernshaw considered the matter briefly, studying the grave expression on Faro's face. "A'right, we'll talk," he said. "But don't pull no stunts, an' don't go figgerin' you kin talk me out of this. My mind's done set."

"It's probably for the best anyway," Faro said.

They went through the house to the kitchen, and Faro took a seat at the long plank table there. Fernshaw sat down across from him and laid his rifle on the table between them, aimed at Faro's chest. Faro chose to ignore the weapon.

"The rope around her arm is a good idea," Faro said. "But it won't be nearly strong enough, not when it, uh, begins. And if I was your son, I don't think I'd want to be the one tied to the other end of that rope when it all starts to happen."

"What kind of damn fool nonsense are you babblin' about?" the old man grumbled.

"Greta's sure a fine-looking woman," Faro said. "You wouldn't believe it just to look at her, would you?"

"Believe what?" Fernshaw demanded.

"That she's a hundred and eleven years old."

"The devil, you say!"

"Her kind holds their age pretty well," Faro went on, "and I've heard it said that there ain't nothing like them between the sheets, if you know what I mean. Most times you couldn't even tell them from a real person. But of course when something sets them off, then that's a different matter entirely. I've been after this one for nigh onto eight months now, but the way things are, I guess she's going to be your problem from here on."

"Damn you, will you get down to the meat of things," Fernshaw stormed. "I cain't make hide nor hair of what you're talkin' 'bout!"

"I'm trying to tell you that your son's fixing to marry himself to a haint, for Chrissake!" Faro explained impatiently.

"A haint?" the old man mumbled.

"They had her locked up safe and sound some months ago in a crazy house in Memphis, but one full moon her powers just got too strong. She went berserk one night, tore that steel door right off its hinges, and got past six guards who tried to stop her."

"That little woman in there?" Fernshaw asked. "She did all that?"

"I saw the place just after she broke out, and it

wasn't pretty," Faro said soberly. "I never seen such a mess of ripped-off heads and bloody carcasses in all my born days. And that door! My God! It was ripped up and twisted around like a pasteboard box. That's when the warden at the crazy house hired me to come after her. All this time, I've just been hoping I could find her and carry her back before somebody got her riled during a full moon"— Fernshaw glanced in alarm at the bright round orb in the sky outside, then back at Faro's face—"but in a way, I'm kind of glad things have turned out like they have," Faro went on. "Nobody wants to die, of course, but I just keep thinking that if I had to take custody of her and those devils got ahold of her on the way back . . . well sir, the thought tends to make getting shot look mighty accommodating."

"My boy Little Bob ain't marryin' up with no crazy gawddamn haint!" Jonah Fernshaw announced with conviction. "We're lucky all this ruckus tonight didn't tip her over the rim!"

"I was half expecting it too," Faro admitted. "It's hard to predict when it's going to happen."

"Soon's I'm done with you, I'm fixin' to run her off this place."

"I'm not sure she would go, not with all these children around here."

"Chil'ren . . . !" Fernshaw exclaimed with alarm. "What's chil'ren got to do with it?"

"I really don't think you want to hear that part of it," Faro stated ominously. "But if she won't go, you could always kill her."

"I will if I hafta," the old man vowed.

"Excellent. Now here's how to go about it. First you get yourself about two pounds of solid silver, as pure as you can buy, and you get somebody to forge it into a knife about eight or ten inches long. Then you gather yourself up some wild garlic and the bark off some fresh sassafrass roots. A couple of bushels of each ought to be enough. Next you take her out to a crossroads at the stroke of midnight, but it's vital that you don't let on to her what you plan to do. After that, you—"

"You've gotta get that haint off my place, mister! Tonight! Right now!"

"Sorry," Faro said.

"I'll blast a hole the size of a fall turnip through you if you don't," Fernshaw threatened.

"I saw that look in her eye a while ago," Faro said. "And take a gander at that moon outside. I hate to say it, but I guess the bullet will do me just fine."

"But I got a passel o' young-uns 'round this place," Fernshaw pleaded. "Hell, eighteen or twenty at least. *You gotta take her off my hands.*"

Faro let a long moment pass as he stared deeply into the old man's eyes. Then finally, in a martyred tone, he reluctantly gave in. "Well, for the sake of the children . . ."

"I know it's around here somewhere," Greta said, stumbling about in the darkness near the edge of the river. "I had just come up from the boat when I heard their dogs coming this way, and I knew I'd better hide it before they got here. There was an old log, half in and half out of the water. I jammed the case in under it and piled some dirt and rocks over the hole. It's just got to be here."

"If we don't find it, I've half a mind to jam you under a log and pile some dirt over you," Faro warned.

"I'm sorry, Faro. I really am!"

"Lady, you can take your 'sorries' and stuff them

where the sun don't shine," he said. "After all the troubles I've gone through to get you and that damn money to New Orleans, you just jumped ship and left me behind to face the music by my own goddamn self. If it wasn't for the money you owed me, I would have left you back there to whelp an army of yard rats for your boyfriend Little Bob!"

"If I hadn't gotten out of there soon, I'm sure I would have gone mad," Greta said. "He beat me up two and three times a day. He called it having to thump the wildness out of me. And all night long he was on and off, on and off. I couldn't get a bit of sleep, and he had me walking bowlegged after the first night."

"I guess folks like them don't have much other way to pass the time," Faro said. "After a year or so there, you might have gotten so you liked it."

"My God! Don't even talk about such a thing!"

After another few minutes of searching, Faro came across a massive fallen log near the edge of the water and called Greta over.

"This is it!" she exclaimed, dropping to her knees and beginning to scrape under it with her hands. In a moment she reached under the log and pulled out the briefcase. "We found it! It's still here!" she shrilled ecstatically.

"Well it's about goddamn time something went right. Open it up."

"Why?" Greta asked. "If the case is still here, the money's bound to be in it. We need to be going before they change their minds and come after us."

"Open it up. I want to see it," Faro said.

Greta opened the case and tilted the lid back out of the way. Faro knelt by her side, and for a moment he just stared down at the neat stacks of bills inside.

It made him feel better just looking at all that money.

"All right," Faro said. "Let's go. We'll stay on the river until we're sure we're clear of this flock of lunatics. We can take a rest in the next town we come to, and then we'll decide what we want to do after that."

Chapter Fourteen

Greta lay naked on the bed, moaning with pleasure as Faro's hands roamed her body. "I sure have come to enjoy this," she told him softly, "but I still don't know why it has to smell so bad."

"I guess that's the price you pay," Faro said. "Lineament always smells this way."

Her hips and legs were still dappled with bruises, reminders of the punishment Little Bob Fernshaw had inflicted on her, but now after a week, they were starting to fade. For the first few days after their escape from the moonshiners, her body had been nearly crippled with stiffness, so in the first small settlement they came to, Faro purchased some horse lineament to ease her suffering. She had protested in the beginning, before she discovered how much relief the stuff provided. Now she was practically addicted to her twice-daily massages.

Faro spread a fresh splash of the oily liquid on his hands, then fell to work kneading it into the backs of her thighs. She winced occasionally when he passed over an especially tender area, but most of the time she just lay there, groaning in delight.

"It's hard to believe we're so close to the end of our pilgrimage," Greta said. "It seems like years since we left St. Louis."

"Well, believe it," he told her. "New Orleans is just on the other side of that big lake out there. Tomorrow morning we'll catch the ferry across, and then we're home free."

The journey from the Fernshaw farm in the southwest corner of Mississippi to where they were now had been tedious and uneventful. Because Faro had come to distrust both steamboat and railroad travel, their trip had been a monotonous succession of rides in the backs of produce-filled wagons and long walks along dusty country roads. It was slow and discomforting, but both of them felt more anonymous and safe when they stuck to the rural countryside.

When they reached the north shore of Lake Pontchartrain, they came to the mutual agreement that they owed themselves some comfort and leisure, and they certainly had enough money to afford it. Lake Pontchartrain was a huge inland body of water nearly forty miles long and thirty miles wide. On its eastern tip it spilled into the Gulf of Mexico, and it was bordered on its southern side by the city of New Orleans. They checked into the Hotel de Royale, a resort hotel which catered to the whims and fancies of the Louisiana elite. Now that they were so close, there seemed to be no great urgency to complete the last leg of their odyssey.

"The first thing I'm going to do when I get to New Orleans is buy myself a whole new wardrobe,"

Greta said. "Not gaudy, scooped-necked satins like the girls in Memphis picked out for me, and certainly not the drab brown things I used to wear either. I can't wait to have some pretty new dresses with ruffles and lace all over them. And I want hats and shoes and parasols and silk petticoats . . ."

"You'll have to be careful not to spend the whole fortune before Anthony Winchell even gets a look at it," Faro laughed.

"He'll be surprised by the changes in me," Greta said.

"And pleased with them too, without a doubt. The next time he crawls between the sheets with you, he'll think he's died and gone to heaven."

"Let's don't talk about that," she said. The mere mention of sexual matters put a damper on her cheerful mood.

Over the past week, Faro had not laid a finger on his young traveling companion except to tend to her various injuries and ailments. It was odd and occasionally frustrating to see her so frequently naked without being able to take sexual advantage of the situation, but he could clearly see how upsetting the rape on the steamboat and her experiences with Little Bob had been. She showed no apparent interest in continuing the learning experiences they started aboard the *Sweet Beulah,* and Faro made no demands of her. They would be separated in a few days, and then it would be up to Winchell to deal with any on going sexual problems which she might have.

After the massage, Greta went into an adjoining room to bathe and cleanse herself of the rank scent of the lineament. Faro stepped out onto the wide balcony of their third-floor suite of rooms and gazed out over the broad expanse of water before him. The lake was so large and the countryside so level that he couldn't see the southern shore thirty miles away. His mind wandered back more than twenty-five years to the first time he and his father had stayed in the Hotel de Royale and he had delighted in this view.

Scores of gamblers from as far away as Dallas, St. Louis and Atlanta had assembled at the hotel that year for a marathon of poker organized by a New Orleans financier. While thousands of dollars, and sometimes tens of thousands, were changing hands at the turn of a card in the upstairs suites, hosts of lovely ladies paraded their jewels and finery in the dining rooms and ballroom below. Somewhere on the grounds music always seemed to be playing, and gentlemanly duels to the death were a daily ritual in the expansive gardens behind the hotel.

The impression which that single magic week had made on Faro was immeasurable. The glittering image of the successful gambler's life had been printed indelibly on his mind, never to be completely destroyed by the harsh realities of the life he lived in later years.

Since then, there had been many, many good times, of course, periods when Lady Luck hovered by his elbow at the tables and some of the most beautiful women in the world hurled themselves into his arms and his bed. But there had been as many bad times, times when he had searched the linings of his clothes for a nickel to buy a beer. The Lady had turned her back to him as often as she had favored him with her presence. It all had a way of averaging out. He had lost as many fortunes as he had won, left as many ladies as he had loved.

Things were no longer quite the same at the Hotel de Royale. The rooms and furnishings were just as lavish, the food just as good and the wine just as expensive. But if a person cared to look closely enough, it was possible to detect a few encroaching signs of neglect and deterioration. The outside walls had gone too long without a fresh coat of paint and were beginning to peel in a few small places. The gardens were not as large nor as beautiful, and their brick walkways needed repair. The tall, nude maiden in the back portico no longer bathed her polished stone body with cascades of water from the alabaster pitcher she held. There was no music anymore.

During the first few days of that week of gambling years ago, A. B. Blake had sailed on a crest of good fortune, winning nearly thirty thousand dollars in half a dozen high-stakes games. But perhaps there could have been a valuable lesson to be learned then if Faro had been mature enough to take heed. The night before they were to leave, his father lost every cent of his winnings in one thirty-minute encounter with a rum smuggler from Mobile. The following morning he had to borrow money from a friend to pay his bill at the hotel. Yet Faro could still recall that A. B. left the affair reveling in the good times he had enjoyed rather than grieving for the fortune which had slipped through his fingers.

Only now did Faro finally understand that the enjoyment was what the whole thing was supposed to have been about from the start.

Greta returned from her bath with a light robe around her shoulders and a towel wrapped around her damp hair. "Why don't you go out for a drink or something?" she suggested. "It's going to take me at least an hour to do my hair, and I think I'd like to take a nap before I start to dress for dinner. Maybe you can hustle yourself up some virtueless maiden to while away the time with."

"I suppose I could use a couple of belts of bourbon." Faro grinned at her. "Among other things."

"Come back for me at seven," she said.

The bartender in the vacant hotel bar was a woman in her early fifties, a lovely lady despite the wrinkles at the corners of her eyes and the traces of gray in her auburn hair. She might have been one of the young lovelies at that legendary *fête* here at the Hotel de Royale twenty-five years before.

She poured his bourbon for him, then hesitated on her side of the bar, trying to gauge whether he wanted conversation or solitude. He tasted his drink and gave her a noncommittal smile. It didn't really matter much to him either way.

"I don't believe I've seen you in here before," she offered. She spoke with a rich Creole accent, though her appearance scarcely indicated such a heritage.

"I just checked in last night," Faro said.

"Heading to New Orleans?"

Faro nodded. "Tomorrow or the next day," he said.

She seemed to sense that he didn't want to talk about himself or his business in the area. "I'm from New Orleans myself," she told him. "I've lived there most of my life. I grew up in Ohio, but I made my way down the river before the war, and I never had much urge to go back again except to visit."

"I like this part of the country quite a bit, except during the hottest summer months. Then I can't tolerate the mosquitoes."

"There's no way to live with them unless you can make a joke out of it like the natives do," she agreed. "Would you like to hear some mosquito jokes?"

"No. Please." Faro grinned. "I bet there haven't been any new ones written in the past fifty years."

Somehow Faro felt completely at ease with this woman. Though her figure was still strikingly full, he felt no great compulsion to lead toward any sort of sexual innuendoes or propositions. She had an air about her of a woman who had been around—perhaps as a prostitute or a madame in one of the famous New Orleans brothels—and sometimes he could relax more fully in the company of such women than with any other.

Their talk meandered over a number of topics, including the decline in the hotel's business, the growth of towns and settlements in the area and the rise in shipping traffic on the lake. All the time that they were talking, Faro kept getting the feeling that her eyes were wandering over the features of his face more intently than necessary, as if she might be trying to memorize every line and detail of his appearance.

Finally, in the midst of their casual conversation, she blurted out, "Is there any chance in the world that your name is Faro Blake?"

"As a matter of fact it is," he replied, gazing back at her curiously. To the best of his recollection, they had never met before a few minutes ago.

She laughed out loud with delight and took his hand up off the bar to give it a warm kiss. "I'm not offended that you don't recognize me," she assured him. "It's been so many, many years. And probably my name won't mean any more to you than my face. It's Elsa. Elsa Peabody."

Faro puzzled for a moment. Her name was familiar, though he could hardly place it in time. He sensed that once they had been very close.

"I remember the year we met," she said, "because

177

it was just a few months after my husband was killed. It was 1855. You were thirteen and I was . . . well . . . a few years older."

It was beginning to come back to Faro, like the details of a long-forgotten dream. And an erotic dream at that.

"My husband had left me rather well off, but still the money couldn't relieve the grief I felt when he died. After a few months of mourning, I decided that travel might help me return to the world of the living. So I booked passage on a steamboat and started down the Mississippi. On the boat I found myself turning away from every man who tried to show me any attention. But I did make one male friend, the son of a riverboat gambler. I thought surely he would be safe company . . ." An intimate smile crossed her features.

Faro was also grinning broadly. The whole thing was coming back to him now. "If I recall correctly," he teased, "the matter of safety might have been in question on both sides of the acquaintance."

"It was probably mostly my doing," she admitted. "But God! I was so lonely, so in need of comfort from another human being. You were fresh, and young, and nice."

"And ready," Faro added with a laugh.

"For years after that I kept telling myself that I should feel guilty about what happened," Elsa said. "I actually seduced a thirteen-year-old boy, for heaven's sake! But I don't think I ever did feel much real guilt about it. I just remembered those nights together as so special. You didn't really seem thirteen."

"I guess I was kind of mature for my age," Faro said. "I did some fast growing up during those first years on the river. And after meeting you, I really

178

thought I was a man of the world. It took a couple of good wallopings from my old man to bring me back to reality." He paused to consider things a moment, then said, "But if I remember correctly, you were rolling in money back then. Your husband left you a fortune, didn't he? What happened? Why are you here in this place pouring drinks now?"

"The war." Elsa shrugged. "I had six good years in New Orleans, but my money was in cotton and steamboats, and a year after Fort Sumter, I was broke. I let an exiled French count keep me for a couple of years, and after I left him, I just naturally drifted into a similar line of business. I put in my time in some of the finest stables in New Orleans, but finally I met that one good man that most women spend their whole lives looking for. He was the *maître d'hôtel* here at the Royale, and after we got married, I came to work here."

"Damn. I love a happy ending!" Faro smiled.

"It has been happy," Elsa said, "but only because I busted my tail making it that way. After all those years I spent flat on my back under every stranger who had the price of admission in his pocket, I learned what a good man was really worth. And when I met this one, I swore come hell or a hurricane, I was going to keep him."

"That's smart," Faro noted.

Elsa smiled. "You tend to learn a thing or two over the years. All those years in New Orleans, the thing that always scared me the most was the thought of growing old alone. But now I'm not afraid anymore. I have Enrique and I know what he's worth to me."

After a few more drinks in the bar, Faro returned to the suite and waited while Greta dressed for dinner. All during the meal he was quiet and pensive, but if his young companion noticed, she made no mention of it. When they finished eating he sent her back to their room while he took a solitary stroll through the hotel gardens, smoking the day's last cheroot.

Something didn't feel quite right about where he was and what was going on, but he found it impossible to identify the cause of his uneasy mood. There was something about being alone in a peaceful garden at night. . . .

Chapter Fifteen

"This, my dear Greta, is Bourbon Street!" Faro announced, sweeping his arm expansively before them. "For the past hundred and fifty years, these cobblestones beneath our feet have witnessed princesses and pirates alike rubbing shoulders here on the streets of the French Quarter."

"Oh my!" Greta said. She seemed more alarmed than impressed by the incredible mix of people who packed the narrow thoroughfare in front of them.

After crossing Lake Pontchartrain on the steam-powered ferry early that morning, they had hired a carriage on the north side of the city to bring them here to the most notorious district of New Orleans. En route to the French Quarter, Greta had instructed the driver to stop at a telegraph office, where she had sent off a coded message to Anthony Winchell announcing that she had arrived safely in New Orleans with the money.

People were hustling in all directions around them. Sweating black laborers jostled their way freely past aristocratic businessmen, sailors and eager young men bargained openly with gaudy streetwalkers, and drunks staggered through the throng like landlubbers on the pitching decks of a seagoing schooner. About every third building seemed to house a drinking establishment, most of which were equipped with a barker near the front door to advertise the entertainment and spirits available inside. For Faro, it was a beckoning, exciting environment, but Greta seemed to hold a different opinion of the scene around them.

"And you say we're going to stay *here* until Anthony arrives?" she asked incredulously. "Since you're a gambler, what would you say our chances are of surviving until then?"

"It's a good place to disappear when that kind of thing is necessary," Faro told her. "Besides, I love it here in the Quarter. And I think you will too, once you get used to it. After all, what's the use of coming to New Orleans if you don't find any excitement?"

"This isn't excitement," Greta insisted. "This is pandemonium. This is unrestrained chaos!"

"Come on. You'll feel better once we check into our rooms and get out of this mob for a while. The place we're going to stay is in a quieter part of the Quarter. I think you'll like it better." He picked up their suitcases and started forward, shoving a pathway through the crowd for Greta to follow.

They had covered no more than a block when an aggressive barker latched onto Faro's sleeve, determined to lure him inside for a drink and a glimpse of the floor show. "C'mon. Give it a try, sport," the barker pestered. "Our girls'll show you somethin' you can tell your grandsons about when you get too old to have any fun anymore!"

"Maybe later," Faro said, pulling on his arm and trying to move on.

The barker, a six-foot, two-hundred pounder with a crooked, jackal's grin, had somehow identified Faro as a good prospect and was determined not to let him escape. He kept his grip firmly on Faro's upper arm and announced, "Special just for you 'cause I like you, sport. You buy the first drink an' the house buys the second. You ever seen a lady drink out of a beer bottle *without usin' her mouth?* It's a sight no adventuresome gentleman like yourself should miss out on."

Faro heard Greta gasp in alarm behind him. He turned to face the barker nose to nose. "I'm not by myself, *sport,*" he said sternly. "Now let go of my arm so that the young lady and I can be on our way."

"Hell, she can go in with you. Nobody won't care!"

Faro dropped the suitcases he was carrying to the sidewalk and reached across with his right hand. His fingers located the tender muscle between the thumb and the index finger of the barker's hand and gave it a punishing squeeze.

The man roared out in pain as he let go of Faro's arm and staggered back in surprise. The shitty grin melted from his face and he swung wildly at Faro with his right fist. Faro parried the blow with his left forearm, doubled his opponent up with a right to the midsection, and sent him to his knees with a solid left cross to the ear.

"Is it starting to get through to you now that I don't want to go inside your goddamn saloon?" Faro snarled.

The barker was gasping for breath and a trickle of blood was coming out of his right ear. He looked up at Faro with cold malice in his eyes and bellowed out, "Marco! Jake! I need some help out here!"

"Oh shit!" Faro mumbled. He turned to face the door, realizing what was going to come pouring out of there in a few seconds. As the two mountainous bruisers came stomping out of the saloon, Faro ran his hand inside his jacket. But the barker saw what he was up to and grabbed his arm before he could draw the Reids's.

Faro clipped the barker across the chin with the point of his boot, eliminating him permanently from the fight, but by then the two hulking bouncers were on top of him. One staggered Faro back with a stunning blow to the jaw, and the other grabbed his right arm before he had a chance to strike back. When Faro swung his left arm around for an ineffective punch, the other bouncer grabbed it and held on. A way parted in the crowd of onlookers as the two men hauled him toward a nearby alley. Faro glanced back once in time to see Greta being swallowed up in the throng of people who shoved along after them.

Seconds later a single shot, not much louder than a large firecracker, cracked out from the alley. There was the sound of male voices cursing one another, a few heavy thumps, and the clatter of metal garbage cans crashing against each other.

Greta was waiting, teary and desperate, by the entrance to the saloon when Faro returned to her a minute later. He was bleeding from his right nostril and from a cut at the corner of his mouth, and his suit coat and shirt were ripped halfway off his body. He had lost his hat somewhere in the confusion.

"Oh Faro!" Greta gasped. "What . . . ?"

"Goddamnit, don't ask!" he growled. He stopped by the downed barker, who was just beginning to come to again, and stared down at him angrily. As the man's head lolled from side to side and his eyes began to flutter open, Faro's foot raised and his heel hovered over his victim's face. "Aw, what's the fucking use!" he decided at last, lowering his foot again. Then, retrieving the suitcases he had been carrying earlier, he said, "Come on, Greta. Let's get out of here before those two in the alley start to come around."

It took them nearly twenty minutes to cover the ten additional blocks to the Ironwood House, the boarding house where Faro usually stayed when he was in New Orleans. On the way there, Faro explained that the proprietor of the place was a man named Simon Butcher, a peg-legged ex-steamboat pilot and an old friend of Faro's father. Many years before, A. B. Blake had saved Butcher's life during a shootout with a drunken band of rowdies on the Vicksburg levee, and ever since that time Faro had been the recipient of Butcher's bountiful gratitude.

The Ironwood House was an antiquated, three-story brick structure with ornate cast-iron balconies overhanging the street on the upper two levels. As soon as Faro and Greta entered the front door, a massive form came hurtling across the vestibule toward them. Greta stumbled back in terror, wondering if she was going to witness a repeat of the brutal scene outside the saloon. But this time Faro met the onslaught with smiles, exchanging only handshakes and hearty slaps on the back with his attacker.

"Simon, you damned old stump jumper!" Faro exclaimed. "How in the hell are you, anyway?"

"If things were any better," Simon Butcher replied, "I just don't think I could stand it!" He was a tall, barrel-chested man in his early sixties. A neatly trimmed, steel gray beard covered the lower half of his face, and he wore an ancient captain's cap on top of his head. "But look at you, Faro," he exclaimed. "Damn your eyes, boy, I just can't let you loose on the streets by yourself anymore, can I?"

"I never am sure I'm in New Orleans until I've shed a little blood," Faro said, dabbing at the corner of his mouth with the cuff of his ruined jacket.

"And caused more than a little to be shed, too, I'll wager." Butcher's glance strayed past Faro to the vicinity of the front door, and he asked, "Who is this young filly? Is she with you?"

"The way I look, she might not be too anxious to admit it," Faro said, "but we came here together. Miss Greta Wimbley, meet my and my Daddy's old friend, Simon Butcher."

"I'm very glad to meet you, Mr. Butcher," Greta said. Reluctantly she placed her hand in the old man's massive paw and shook hands.

"It's a pleasure, Miss Wimbley," Butcher assured her. "If you're traveling with this here tinhorn upstart, then you can be sure of a welcome here as long as you want to stay."

As they were talking, a lovely young black woman in a white dress came out of a back room and stopped near the doorway. When Faro's eyes came to rest on her, he asked in amazement, "Could that be Dominique?"

"None other," Butcher confirmed with a proud grin.

"She's fleshed out a right smart since the last time I saw her," Faro noted.

"Come here, darling, and say hello to my friends," Butcher instructed. The young woman came to his side and greeted the two new arrivals with smiles of welcome.

"Is this your, uh, daughter?" Greta asked hesitantly.

"Lord no!" Butcher said with a loud laugh. "She's my wife! She was just a child when I bought her seventeen years ago from an old hoodoo man who figgered on turning her into an obeah woman when she growed up. I brought her up like I wanted her, and when she come to the right age, I married her."

"He was going to turn her into an 'obeah woman?'" Greta asked. "That has something to do with voodoo, doesn't it?"

"Exactly. He figured she had the right qualifications, but I thought it wasn't no life for a pretty young gal, skulking about in the dark, burying snake bones and High John the Conqueror Root at folks' doorsteps. So I paid him some money and he turned her over to me to raise."

"What in heaven's name would be the right qualifications for a child to become a voodoo woman?" Greta asked.

"Dominique's got three nipples," Faro explained.

"That's God's own truth," Butcher confirmed. "Show her, Dominique."

Without hesitation, the young woman unbuttoned the front of her dress and pulled back the right side, revealing one full, ebony breast. The sight was so startling that Greta didn't even have the presence of mind to be embarrassed. About three inches to the left of Dominique's right nipple was another one, as large and neatly formed as the first. She let Faro and Greta have a good look, then primly closed her clothing again.

"A thing like that's supposed to be powerful juju to these black magic folks," Butcher said, "but I don't hold no store by all that hocus-pocus stuff. Once an old man tried to slip a jar of snake eggs under my front doorstep because I wouldn't let them borrow Dominique for one of their ceremonies. I made him sit down on the step and eat the whole jar full, and after that they pretty much left us alone."

After visiting for a few more minutes, Dominique showed the two new arrivals to the third floor rooms where they would be staying. Faro had decided that he and Greta should take separate rooms so that Anthony Winchell would have no suspicions about their sleeping arrangements once he arrived. It would have suited Faro even more to simply take his money and go his own way, but Greta persuaded him to stay with her at least until Winchell came. He didn't really mind the delay. He would enjoy the visit with his old friend.

After peeling off his suit and throwing open the French doors which led to the balcony, Faro piled down on his bed and began to contemplate the uses to which he would soon start putting his five thousand dollars.

Chapter Sixteen

It was three in the afternoon, and both Faro and Simon Butcher were already half tight. They were sitting in the shady, enclosed courtyard behind Butcher's boarding house, sipping mint juleps and talking about times long past. Faro was as familiar with most of Butcher's yarns as he was with the faces on a deck of cards, but he still enjoyed hearing them again, slightly changed and embellished as they always were.

"Yessir, boy," Butcher drawled, "next to Captain Noel Hooter and my own brother Pete, your daddy was likely the best friend I ever had in my life. As a rule, I never had much use for gambling men and their types, but A. B. Blake was a man you could count on. Take you for example. There was never any proof that he had truly whelped you all those years before, but he still took you in and did the best job he could raising you up."

"I don't have any complaints about the kind of life he gave me," Faro said. "But you know, Simon, I have to wonder sometimes how different things would have been if mama hadn't died and if I hadn't come to live on the river when I was ten years old. It's hard to picture myself behind a plow horse, making a crop on some farm in Kentucky, but I guess that's where I would be today if things hadn't turned out like they did."

"I can't say it's a life I'd envy," the old man noted, "though I suppose some folks cotton to it."

"After all the years you spent on the move," Faro asked, "how did you finally bring yourself to settle down here?"

"It wasn't that hard for me," Butcher said. "When the war started, I could see that the old days I loved so much were gone forever. I tried for a while to be a pilot on a Confederate supply boat, but I didn't take to the life. I never had owned no slaves, so I really didn't feel like the war was much of my concern, and there was something that went against my nature about hauling loads of cannon shot and gunpowder from one place to another just so men in different colors of jackets could use it to kill one another. When the Yankees blasted the *Diane* out from under me back in sixty-two, I just swam to shore and started south. I knew I was safe from conscription because even as hard up as the Confederate Army got for men near the end, they weren't going to take no old man with a wooden leg.

"But things have been pretty good for me here," Butcher went on. "I started getting used to the life after the first couple of years, and then I found myself wondering why I hadn't done something like this a long time ago. I've got this place, and I've got Dominique, and I have enough friends drop by from time to time to hear me rattle on that I don't generally get bored. It's a better life than a lot I could imagine."

Things had been quite peaceful during the two days that Faro and Greta had been in New Orleans. They had even risked venturing out into the streets a few times. Faro had accompanied Butcher on some drinking expeditions and visits with friends, and Dominique had taken Greta to a dressmaker of her acquaintance for some fittings. Greta had even surprised Faro by heading out twice on her own to go shopping.

The casual conversation of the two men was interrupted when Dominique came out into the courtyard and stopped nearby.

"There is a man here," she began in a guarded tone of voice. Faro hadn't told her anything about his and Greta's business, but during the two days they had been here, the young black woman had come to understand quickly enough that they were more or less in hiding. "He was asking about you and your friend," Dominique told Faro, "but I didn't tell him anything."

Faro gave her a quick description of Anthony Winchell, and she confirmed that that was what the stranger looked like.

"Is it trouble?" Butcher asked with concern.

"It's not supposed to be," Faro said. "I wonder if I could meet with him out here in the courtyard and talk a few things over with him before Greta knows he's here?"

"Of course," Butcher said. "And I'll be just inside the kitchen there with my rifle handy in case there's trouble."

"There shouldn't be any, but thanks."

Butcher and his young wife went inside, and a

minute later Winchell came out into the courtyard. As he approached Faro, he exclaimed, "You have no idea what a relief it is to find you here! Every day since the two of you left St. Louis has been unadulterated torment to me."

"Things didn't exactly go smoothly on the way down," Faro said. He was studying Winchell, trying to probe beyond the man's facade for concealed messages.

"Is Greta here with you?" Winchell asked. "Is she all right?"

"She's safe," Faro replied.

"And the, uh, merchandise?"

"Safe."

"Well where are they? I want to see them!"

"Soon," Faro said. "But first we have to talk."

"What could there possibly be to talk about?" Winchell asked. "You've done your job. Now you can go your way as soon as I pay you the five hundred dollars you have coming."

"That's one of the things we have to talk about. On the train, the price went up as soon as I learned what that satchel had in it. I've got five thousand coming now instead of five hundred."

Winchell started to protest, but Faro halted him with an upraised hand. "There's no use arguing about it," he said. "That's my new price, and you're going to pay it. And believe me, I've earned every cent of it along the way."

"All right, Mr. Blake," Winchell agreed reluctantly. "Your services and your silence have undoubtedly been worth the price. What else?"

"I want to know what went on in St. Louis after we left," Faro demanded. "Why was there a private detective on the same train as we were on who knew more about our business than we did? All the way down here I've been wondering if you were trying to pull some kind of doublecross on us, and now's the time for you to convince me that you weren't."

"I can assure you, that is not the case!" Winchell announced indignantly. "Since the moment you left, and even before, things have not been going according to plan. For days now, the prospect of doom has been hanging over my head like a dark cloud. But I stuck it out. I have worked diligently to ensure that—"

"Just tell me what went wrong on your end," Faro said impatiently. "That's the only thing I want to hear right now."

"When Greta and I took the money, we assumed that the theft would not be discovered until the following Monday, which would have given the two of you time to get completely away. But for some unexpected reason, Peter Sylvester decided to stop by the bank Saturday morning, and he discovered the theft at about the same time your train was leaving the station. He looked me up as I was returning from paying you your money, and I was forced to cast the blame on Miss Wimbley much sooner than I had anticipated."

"We had that much figured out already," Faro said. "But where did Turk Bishop come into the picture?"

"I convinced Mr. Sylvester that perhaps we could recover the money and return it to the bank before news of the theft became public. It would have been a much more discreet way of handling the matter. So we hired Mr. Bishop, and we told him that he was being sent to recover a satchel of important documents. But I had no idea he would act so quickly. He checked at the train station and found out when the two of you had left, then he got a fast horse and was able to reach East St. Louis before your train started south. He sent us a message from East St. Louis saying he intended to board the train and look for you. He never contacted us after that."

"The chances of him contacting anybody ever again from this world are pretty slim," Faro said guardedly. "He found out what was in the satchel, too, and he decided to steal it for himself. But he met with misfortune on the way down here."

"We decided something like that must have happened," Winchell said. "By the following week, Mr. Sylvester was forced to turn the matter over to the authorities and to the bonding company. I stayed on with the bank for a few more days, then resigned in apparent disgrace after accepting full responsibility for letting the robbery take place. I knew that would make it much easier for me to disappear if and when I ever heard from Greta again."

"Tell me this, Winchell. Did you ever give my name to the police or to the bonding company?"

"Certainly not! If I had admitted to knowing you, it would have been tantamount to also admitting a knowledge of the robbery itself, which would have placed me in jeopardy."

If that was true, it was a great relief to Faro. He didn't particularly delight in the prospect of having a bank robbery warrant hanging over his head after he parted with these two.

"Does that satisfy your curiosity, Mr. Blake?" Winchell asked impatiently.

"I suppose so," Faro said.

"Do you have any more questions?"

"Not right now."

"Then will you please take me to Greta now. I'd like to see for myself that she and the money are all right."

"I guess what's pleased me most about this whole business," Faro said as he rose to his feet, "is how much trust we've all been able to place in one another! Come on. She's upstairs in her room."

The reunion between Greta Wimbley and Anthony Winchell was a curious one, considering that these were two people who said they intended to marry and spend the rest of their lives together. When Greta opened the door and stepped back to let them in, there were no smiles nor joyous hugs. For the first minute, Winchell merely stood in the doorway, staring at her with more alarm than pleasure.

"I hardly know what to say, Greta," he told her at last. "You look so . . . so different!"

"On the way down here," she explained, "Faro convinced me that a notorious bank robber such as I seem to have become should have more flash and flair about her."

"Is that so," Winchell said, casting Faro a dark glance. "And what else did the gentleman convince you of?"

"For one thing," she replied, "he helped me understand that perhaps I had entered into this 'partnership' of ours without having my eyes fully open concerning the consequences. This hasn't been an easy trip, Anthony. I've learned a lot on the way down here, and I suppose I should warn you that our future relationship might not be quite like you expected."

Winchell's scowl was growing more and more severe as the moments passed, and Faro thought it might be smart for him to finish with his part of this business before they started slugging it out in earnest.

"Listen, folks," he said. "I hate to interrupt such a tender reunion, but as of this moment, my job is finished. If you don't mind, I'm going down to get the briefcase so that you can pay me off. Simon has it hidden somewhere down in his cellar."

He went downstairs in search of their host, and within five minutes he was back upstairs with the briefcase in hand. Simply being in the vicinity of the fortune did much to improve Winchell's mood. He snatched the briefcase from Faro and hurried to the bed.

"I had to take out a couple of hundred dollars for expenses," Greta explained, "but other than that, it's all there."

Winchell fumbled the clasps open and gazed down at the neat stacks of bills, then looked up at the others with an expression of utter joy on his face. "We did it!" he exclaimed. "Up until this very second, I don't think I ever fully believed that we would get away. But we did. Here's the proof!"

"You're going to have plenty of time to pat yourselves on the backs for your great accomplishment," Faro said with a note of impatience in his voice. "But right now, if you don't mind . . ." He nodded his head toward the briefcase, which was opened with its lid toward him. "That's five thousand dollars even."

Winchell picked up one banded stack of bills and started to count, but suddenly a look of confusion replaced the joy on his face. He dropped the bundle back into the briefcase and his hand slid inside his suit coat. Faro realized only a second too late that the banker was going for a gun.

"For both your sakes," Winchell said, "I hope this is some sort of stupid joke you decided to play on me." He was leveling a snub-nosed revolver at them, and judging by the look on his face, he was dangerously close to pulling the trigger.

"Anthony!" Greta said. "Have you gone mad?"

"I am not amused by this," the banker said.

"What is your goddamn problem, Winchell?" Faro asked angrily.

"The money . . . !"

"So what?" Faro said. "It's all there. If you know what's good for you, you'll count out my five thousand and let me be on my way. Then whether or not you decide to split the rest with her is your business."

"All right, Blake!" Winchell stormed. "If you want your money, then you count it out. Here!" He reached down into the briefcase and withdrew a handful of its contents, which he hurled in Faro's direction.

Faro managed to catch just one bundle. The minute he examined it, he realized what the problem was. He raised his eyes to look at Winchell, then shifted his glare in Greta's direction. The bundle he held contained one real twenty-dollar bill on the top and bottom, and the rest was simply newsprint cut to the shape of currency. Winchell hurled the briefcase off the bed and onto the floor.

Winchell sneered at them. "You two must have really taken me for some sort of dimwitted lout! What did you have in mind? To get rid of me and then take all the money for yourselves? Did you have some way figured out to get me blamed for the crime while the two of you were off enjoying yourselves? Just how did you plan to get away with it?"

Greta tried to explain. "Walter, I swear to you—"

"Shut up!" the banker told her. "I don't want to hear your lies. But you know what? I had a plan of my own. When I got my hands on that money—

when I do get my hands on it—I had no intention of taking you with me anyway. Why should I settle for you when a hundred thousand dollars can buy me any woman I want? As for you, Blake, this just makes things that much simpler. I won't feel any obligation to pay you a cent after you tell me where the real money is. And you *will* tell me where it is."

"Look, Winchell, I don't know anything more about what's going on here than you do," Faro said. "But I'd advise you to do a little bit of thinking before you do anything drastic."

"I only have to think about one thing, and that's how to make one of you talk. I'm sure I can find a way."

"But if we were planning this big doublecross, why would we go to the bother of waiting for you to come all the way down to New Orleans?"

"Maybe to kill me like you apparently did Bishop so there wouldn't be any witnesses against you. I don't know why, but I'm sure it had some purpose in your scheme. But you should have given me more credit. Do you think I would come here without any means to defend myself? Now who's going to talk first? Will it be you, Greta?" Winchell grabbed the young woman by the hair and shook her furiously.

"No, Anthony! Please God, no! I don't know where it is! Faro must have taken it!" she yelled at the top of her lungs. With all his might, Winchell backhanded her across the face with the hand that held the gun, sprawling her across the bed and onto the floor beyond. Faro didn't like to see her in such pain, but he was glad of her shrill protests. They would certainly be heard down on the ground floor, which meant Butcher would be coming to their aid very quickly.

"How about it, Blake?" Winchell said, directing

his attention to Faro. "Maybe a couple of bullet holes here and there would refresh your memory."

"If you pull that trigger at all, you son of a bitch," Faro growled, "you'd better shoot to kill."

The banker seemed to realize that threats and violence would not be nearly so effective on a man, so he turned on Greta once more. Keeping Faro covered with the pistol, he walked around the bed to where she lay in a heap on the floor. "Oh please, Anthony! Please!" she pleaded hysterically as he hauled her roughly to her feet. "I swear I don't know what happened to it! Don't hurt me anymore!"

Ignoring her wails, Winchell slammed her against the wall, then drew back his fist and crashed it into her stomach. The breath left her body in one massive rush and she went down again.

"If you've got it," he warned, "then you'd better get around to talking pretty soon. And if it's him who made the switch, then let's just hope he cares enough about you that he won't just stand there and watch me beat you to death!"

Faro's mind was racing like mad, trying to get the whole situation figured out before it was too late. He knew Greta would not be able to stand much more of that kind of punishment without being seriously injured or killed, but Winchell was covering him closely with the revolver. Stupid heroics at this point would probably be fatal.

What had happened to the money? If Greta had made the switch, then perhaps she deserved the beating she was getting now. But where had she had the opportunity to do it and where was the money now? And for that matter, where in the hell was Simon Butcher?

Winchell raised Greta up and batted her across the bed once again. She was close to unconsciousness now, and Winchell acted as if he was actually starting to enjoy brutalizing her. Finally when the banker stepped to the bed and focused his full attention on his female victim for an instant, Faro recognized the only opportunity he was likely to get. As soon as he sprang forward, Winchell began to swing the gun around, but Faro caught his arm and hoisted it up in the air. As they went down, Faro's head glanced off the iron bedpost. A shower of stars raced through his addled consciousness, but somehow he managed to hang onto the arm which held the pistol.

"Greta! Go get Simon!" Faro yelled out. He wasn't sure that she was aware enough to even hear him, but he had an idea that he was going to need some help fairly soon. The rap on the head had sapped his strength, and Winchell was a more powerful man than Faro had given him credit for being. The gun went off as the two of them rolled around clumsily on the floor. Out of the corner of his eye, Faro saw Greta stumbling out the door.

Winchell's hand collided hard with the metal bed and the pistol clattered across the floor. Realizing that, Faro let go of the banker's arm and popped him in the face a couple of times with his fist. Winchell was grabbing and clawing at Faro, fighting almost like a woman, and Faro couldn't get himself in a position to deliver a really telling blow. He could feel his own strength returning, but it was coming slow.

During the scuffle, the banker's arm flailed out and his fingers fastened around the leg of a small table. He swung it around and struck Faro across the back with it, temporarily immobilizing Faro with a surge of pain. Winchell used the instant of relief to scramble across the floor and retrieve his weapon.

"All right, just hold it right there!"

Surprisingly enough, the warning came not from Winchell, but from Simon Butcher, who stood in the doorway across the room with his rifle in hand. Winchell, however, was not ready to give up just yet. As his hand started up to fire the pistol he held, Faro made a grab for it and managed to divert his aim downward just as the gun went off. The bullet slammed into Butcher's wooden leg, snatching it out from under him. As the old man started down, the deafening roar of his rifle filled the room.

Winchell's arm went limp in Faro's grasp and the small weapon spilled from his fingers. Faro turned his head and looked into the banker's incredulous eyes. One of them was soon filled with the blood which trickled down from the bullet hole in his forehead. His body settled slowly sideways to the floor.

"Shit, Simon!" Faro exclaimed. "You could have hit me, snapping off a shot on the way down like that!"

"I wasn't aiming for you!" Butcher answered irritably. "I got him, didn't I, so what are you bitching about?" He pulled his damaged wooden leg around in front of him and examined it, trying to decide whether or not it was still functional. He decided it was and struggled to his feet at the same time that Faro was rising unsteadily.

"Where in the hell were you?" Faro asked. "We were making enough noise up here to wake the dead!"

"I was out back in the goddamn shithouse," the old man explained. "At my age, a man has to go about six times as often as he used to. I didn't hear anything until I started back into the house. Then I heard a couple of shots, and a second later that woman of yours came squawling down the stairs like somebody'd just set her backside afire. Dominique set out for the market about half an hour ago, so she wasn't around either."

Glancing down at the lifeless heap of flesh on the floor at his feet, Faro said, "I've sure got you involved in a mess this time, Simon. I'm sorry to bring this kind of trouble on you."

"It's not much trouble to speak of," Butcher commented.

"Well, we've got ourselves a dead body here that the police are going to want us to account for, and they're sure to be interested in what the fight was all about in the first place. There's plenty about this situation I haven't told you yet, my friend."

"The only way the police are going to be interested in this feller is if they know about him," Butcher said. "And there's ways to make sure they don't."

"Can you arrange that, Simon?" Faro asked hopefully.

"I know people who know people," the old man chuckled. "There wouldn't be too many questions asked if he was found tomorrow morning in an alley down by the docks with his wallet empty. Or we could let him feed the fishes in the river if you prefer."

"It doesn't matter to me," Faro said, "and I guess he's beyond caring. But if he was found on land, at least he would get a proper burial. Greta might prefer that. They were supposed to get married, but after all this, I suspect that things wouldn't have worked out between them."

After a couple of minutes Faro started to feeling a little better. His head was throbbing dully where it had struck the bed, and his back felt stiff and bruised, but he knew he would live. He followed

Butcher downstairs to tell Greta that things were all right and that Winchell was dead.

After looking in a couple of the rooms on the ground floor of the house and not locating his young companion, Faro began to get a bad feeling about what was going on. Soon Butcher joined in the search and they went over every room on the first floor. Faro went out into the courtyard and checked it carefully, then he rejoined his friend in the kitchen.

"She must have been so scared that she just skedaddled," Butcher suggested. "Probably when she calms down, she'll come on back."

"She's skedaddled, all right," Faro said with disgust. "But I wouldn't tell Dominique to set a place for her at the supper table. I've got a feeling that I've been slickered good and proper this time, Simon."

"The coffee's on," the old man said. "You pour us a couple of cups while I fetch us something to spike it with. It's time you told me why I just killed a man in the upstairs of my own house."

Chapter Seventeen

Faro awoke with a dull pain in his temples and at the base of his skull. He was sweaty and stiff, and he hated the sunlight which poured into his room through the thin curtains over the French doors. This morning he would have to pay some dues for what he had done last night.

Early the previous day he and Simon Butcher had set out to find some trace of Greta, but their efforts had been futile. No one seemed to have noticed her leaving the boarding house, and none of the employees at the hotels they checked had seen a woman matching her description. By the end of the day when they stopped by one of Butcher's favorite saloons for a drink, they were tired, hot and disgusted. One drink had become many, and by the time Faro realized what was going on, dawn was lighting up the eastern sky as he and Simon staggered through the empty streets of the French Quarter on their way back to the Ironwood House.

With some effort he rose from the bed, pulled on his trousers and went over to pull the bell cord which hung by the door. He took a cheroot from his jacket pocket and studied it a moment, then put it aside, deciding not to light it until Dominique brought the coffee.

The problem with looking for Greta was that he couldn't guess with any degree of confidence where she might have gone when she ran out of the boarding house the day before yesterday, nor what she would do now that she was on her own. She was the one who had switched the money. He was convinced of that, but where had she pulled the switch, and where was the money now? The possibilities seemed practically limitless, starting in St. Louis and covering the entire length of their route to New Orleans.

It was possible that she might have had precisely this sort of thing in mind from the very start. She could have prepared the phony bundles before she and Winchell even stole the real money. At some point while the two of them were separated, she could have stashed the currency in a safe place, then boarded the train as if everything was going according to plan. But something told Faro that that was not what happened. She seemed as determined as Faro to reach New Orleans, which would not have made much sense if she left the money behind in St. Louis.

Along the way, there had been many occasions when the two of them were separated for hours at a time, affording her with ample time to cut the currency-sized strips of newsprint, band them up and make the substitution. She could have done it on the train, at Nell's, or even in her cabin on the steamboat. But then what had she done with the real money? It was certainly not among the things she left behind. He had made sure of that.

There was only one fact about which he was absolutely sure. He had not given Miss Greta Wimbley nearly enough credit for treachery and superb acting skills. Even at the moment when Winchell was beating her horribly, she had delivered a fine performance. And like any consummate actress, she had managed to steal the show at the end.

After a number of drinks the previous evening, Simon Butcher started finding the whole business irritatingly funny, and he told Faro that it was probably what he deserved for getting himself involved in such a boondoggle in the first place. He advised Faro to cut his losses and return to the line of work he knew best. There was always plenty of gambling activity going on in a wide-open place like New Orleans, and Butcher had the contacts to get Faro into a game whenever he was ready.

But this business with Greta continued to grate at Faro. He could not rid himself of the feeling that she was still somewhere close by, flaunting her victory over him with her continuing presence in New Orleans. He knew that to Greta, this city represented all the glamour and adventure that she had craved, and it was the gateway to all the exciting places where she planned to enjoy her new wealth. She could be thinking that all she had to do was wait him out. Eventually he would grow tired of looking for her and leave, and then she could go about enjoying her new life at her leisure. But Faro disliked the idea of being duped about as much as he hated anything in the world.

When he heard a light rap on his door, Faro called out, "Come in." Dominique entered carrying a mug and an earthenware pitcher filled with coffee.

"Good afternoon," she said with a tolerant smile. She was wearing a bright print dress which accentuated her full, supple figure, and Faro thought she looked exceedingly lovely today. It never hurt to look, even when the fruit was forbidden.

"Is it that late?" Faro asked.

"I just finished washing the midday dishes," she said. "Did you sleep well?"

"Once I finally got around to it"—Faro grinned— "I slept like the dead."

"Simon told me your search for the young lady was unsuccessful," Dominique said. She poured a mug of coffee from the pitcher and gave it to Faro, then went over and pulled back the curtains. Faro turned away from the increased glare of the midday sun. "I'm sorry things are not going well for you."

"I hate like hell to admit it," Faro said, "but it sure seems like that little wench has gotten the best of me."

"It's a shame about all her pretty dresses, too," Dominique noted. "She seemed so happy about them."

"Her dresses?" Faro asked. "What dresses are you talking about?"

"The ones she was having Madame Paulette make for her. She was to have picked them up just today if she had not run off like she did."

As soon as the idea entered his head, Faro recognized it as a ridiculous notion. After everything else that had happened, surely she would not have the audacity to go by and pick up her new clothing on schedule. And yet she was proving herself to be quite a bold lady, and as unpredictable as hell. . . .

He lay in an alley with a half-filled bottle of rum cradled in his arms. His clothes were ragged and filthy, but they were no more dirty than his face and arms. A shapeless felt hat was pulled far down over his face. Nobody bothered him. He looked too drunk to move and too poor to rob. Across the street from the alley was a small, neat shop with a sign in the window which introduced its proprietress as MADAME PAULETTE, FRENCH DRESSMAKER.

Faro reached down and scratched his left side, wishing there had been time to delouse these clothes before wearing them. But he could tolerate the nuisance for a few hours, he decided, especially if any positive results came from today's vigil.

Faro kept reminding himself how faint the chance was that Greta would decide to return here and pick up her dresses. On the surface, it would be foolhardy for her to even consider doing such a thing. But he remembered how longingly she had talked about stylishly outfitting herself and becoming a lady. There was a small chance, and at the moment it was the only one he had.

He scooted around in the alley, trying to find a more comfortable position on the lumpy cobblestones. Then he pulled the cork from the rum bottle and took a healthy slug. While his attention was momentarily diverted, he heard the bell on the shop door tinkle, but he glanced up only in time to see the back of a female form go inside. Some instinct sent a rush of excitement through him. It was like the feeling he'd had a few rare times in his life as cards began to fall around a poker table and he sensed that this was the hand when the stakes began to soar. The next few minutes passed with infuriating slowness.

At last a woman came out of the shop and stepped into the edge of the street. Faro's hopes for success dissolved when he realized that it wasn't Greta. Instead of walking away, the woman hailed a passing horse-drawn taxi and instructed the driver to stop in front of the shop. Then she went back inside and began carrying out a variety of flat boxes, which she carefully loaded in the back of the carriage. When all the boxes were loaded, she reentered the shop.

When the woman came back out again, someone was with her, but the carriage was in the way and Faro couldn't see who it was. Suddenly he began to get that feeling again. He rose to his feet, left the alley and began shuffling down the street, trying to appear inconspicuous as he moved to a place where he could get a look at the second woman. After a brief conversation, one of the women climbed into the carriage and muttered some instructions to the driver.

As the carriage moved past him, Faro pulled his hat down farther over his face and raised his head. From the back of the carriage a pair of female eyes moved over him without recognition. It was Greta!

For the first few blocks Faro had trouble keeping up with the horse-drawn taxi. He sprinted down the middle of the street, ignoring the curious stares of the people he raced past. Finally he saw another carriage about a block ahead, and after Greta's carriage had passed it, he raced up to it and leaped into the backseat.

The driver turned to Faro with a furious scowl on his face and said, "Get out of my hack, you goddamn rummy! You'll stink the seats up so bad no decent folks will ride with me!"

Faro fished in his pockets and produced a crumpled twenty-dollar bill. "Would this convince you to tolerate my company for a while?" he asked.

The driver eyed the bill greedily. It was probably as much as he made during a good week. "I don't s'pose you stink no worse than Miss Lila, my horse," he conceded.

"Do you see that carriage up there?" Faro asked hurriedly. Greta's carriage had already gained a full block on them. "The whole twenty's yours if you follow it to wherever it's going!"

The driver popped Miss Lila on the rump with his reins, and within a short time he had narrowed the distance between the two vehicles to a few dozen feet. Faro settled back on the seat with a broad grin on his face as he clawed at an itch on his stomach. Things were finally starting to go his way.

The look on Greta's face told the whole story when she opened the door of her hotel room and saw Faro standing in the hall. He smiled and waited for the instant of panic to pass.

"Faro!" she sputtered. "You're alive! You're all right! I thought Anthony had killed you!"

"Not quite," he told her quietly.

"I heard the gun go off when I ran out, and I thought you were dead," she said. "Then when I got downstairs I heard more shots. I was scared to death. All I could think about was to run away before he killed me too."

"Well, it looks like you had a pretty good idea where to run to," he noted. When he started forward, Greta took a reluctant step backward so he could enter her room.

"Oh this," Greta mumbled. Her hotel accommodations here were equally as luxurious as the suite they had occupied at the Hotel de Royale. The room they were in was a spacious, comfortable sitting room, and through an open doorway Faro glimpsed an elegant bedroom. She offered no explanations about how she had arranged such quarters, and Faro chose not to force the issue for the present.

After finding out where she was staying, Faro had gone back to Simon Butcher's to clean up and change clothes before returning here. He had packed his belongings and brought them along, but had left them with the desk clerk before coming up to confront Greta. A vague plan was taking shape in his mind, but he realized that he would have to learn more about what was going on before he made any definite decisions. Dealing with this highly deceptive young woman would be a delicate matter from here on.

"I know you must be wondering what's going on, Faro," Greta told him nervously. "I suppose you think I've been trying to trick you to get out of paying you your five thousand dollars."

"If you thought I was dead, I can understand why you didn't want to come back to Simon's," Faro said. He kept his voice level, permitting no trace of anger to show in his tone.

"I'm going to be honest with you now, Faro," Greta said. She crossed the room to a sofa and sat down, then patted the place beside him. "Come over and sit with me, Faro. I'll tell you everything. Then I think you'll understand all the suspicious things I've been doing lately." He joined her on the sofa.

"It wasn't until after we had taken the money and I was already on the train that I started to realize what a serious thing Anthony and I had done," she began. "Up until then it was simply this grand, giddy dream that he and I had talked about for days and days. But when that man on the train broke into my compartment, knocked me around and took the satchel from me, it struck me all of a sudden how real it all was. And at the same time, I realized that there wasn't anybody that I could truly trust. I didn't know you and certainly didn't feel that I could trust you at the time, and I started to understand that I probably couldn't even trust Anthony, the man with whom I had committed the crime and the man I was supposed to marry. What he said in my room a couple of days ago simply confirmed what I had already come to know.

"I decided that I would have to take care of myself because nobody else was going to, and that is when I started planning what I wanted to do. The first step was to get the money out of my possession and to a place where it would be safe until all my other difficulties were settled."

"And that's when you decided to substitute cut paper for the real money," Faro said.

"Exactly. I did it while we were in your friend's bordello in Memphis. During the times when I was alone in my room, I cut the newspapers up, banded them with a real bill on either side, and filled the briefcase with them. Then I put the real money in a box, and when you sent me ahead to board the steamboat, I had my driver stop at a post office on the way. I mailed the money to myself care of general delivery here in New Orleans."

"That was very clever of you, Greta," Faro told her.

"It almost backfired on me a number of times," she admitted. "From there on, every time that case was opened I was sure you would discover what I had done. You would have only had to take out one bundle and look at it closely, but you never did. When we reached New Orleans, I went to the post office and picked up the package, then I came here and rented this room. It was like my insurance policy. I still wasn't sure what I wanted to do or what might happen to me, but I did know that as long as I had the money in my possession, anybody could take it from me whenever they decided to do so. You could have, or Anthony could when he arrived.

"But please believe me, Faro," she said urgently. "I never really had it in my mind to rob you! You saved my life on the steamboat, and you saved me from those horrible moonshiners later. Then when we got here, you saved me again from Anthony Winchell. You never tried to take all the money for yourself, and you deserve the five thousand dollars I promised you. And you shall have it, at least that much!"

"I'm glad to hear you say that, Greta," Faro told her. "I guarantee you, the trouble would have started up worse than ever if you felt any different. But what did you mean when you said 'at least that much?'"

"I could pay you right now, and we could go our separate ways," she said, "or we could stay together and share all the money." Her voice became quieter as she made the proposal. She glanced away from him, as if in embarrassment. "On the *Sweet Beaulah* I got a taste of what life could be like with a man like you," she went on, "and it didn't take me long to realize that being married to Anthony Winchell could never compare to that. It was marvelous! It was exciting and fulfilling, and when you held me in your arms and made love to me, I felt more like a woman than I ever had in my entire life."

"You know enough about me to know that I've never stayed with a woman on any sort of permanent basis," Faro noted.

"But perhaps you've never been lured with such tempting bait," she said brightly.

Faro grinned. "That's true enough. You and a share in one hundred thousand dollars . . . A man would have to be a blamed idiot to say 'no' off the cuff to an offer like that."

"Think about it, Faro," Greta said, taking his hand warmly. "I don't expect you to give me an answer right away, but perhaps if we spent a little more time together, I could convince you how enjoyable it could be." She slid over closer to him on the sofa and grazed her lips lightly across his. "As a matter of fact, if you're available for a little gentle persuasion right now . . ."

"When I'm not available for that anymore," Faro chuckled, "is the day the undertaker had better start measuring me for a pine box."

Chapter Eighteen

Faro stood by the open window, staring out at the broad avenue which ran past the hotel. In the moonlight, the towering cyprus trees along the street seemed to hover over the thoroughfare like winsome giants, sighing out their loneliness as the nighttime breezes filtered through their branches. The sights and sounds and smells of the gentle night filled Faro with a comfortable sense of peace.

He felt good. Things had been going much better than he had expected. During the previous afternoon and evening, Greta had dedicated herself to proving how enjoyable a relationship with her could be, and he found himself thinking that if that was the sort of thing he could expect all the time, then a future spent with her might not be such an undesirable proposition. They had eaten and drunk and frolicked in bed until their bodies and senses were utterly sated from the deluge of pleasures.

Greta was sprawled out on the huge bed, lost in deep slumber for the past few hours. But as tired as he was, Faro had slept very little during the long night. His mind was too busy digesting all the things which had happened in the past three days, and going over what was yet to come. Quite obviously it was all too good to be true.

After standing at the window for several minutes, Faro returned to the bed and lay down beside Greta. She stirred slightly, brushing the sheet aside with her arm. Faro studied her pale body for a while, then reached out and began running his fingers lightly up the inside of one of her thighs.

"Unnhh . . ." she whimpered faintly. Her immediate reaction, even asleep, was to part her legs slightly. She began to wake up as his caresses reached the silken lips which surrounded her crevice. They were still slippery with the dampness of their earlier lovemaking. "Oh, Faro," she sighed.

His fingers wandered softly across her belly, circled the nipple of each of her breasts, and started back down again. Her eyes started to open as if their lids were weighted. "I'm asleep," she protested vaguely.

"Not anymore, you aren't," he teased.

"But I want to be. We did it so many times already."

"So what can once more hurt?" he asked. She reacted only slightly as his fingertip grazed her clitoris and slid inside her. Her eyes closed again as if she believed she might be able to sleep through it all. Faro thought that would be fine with him if she could manage it.

He didn't bother trying to get her aroused. As soon as his penis swelled to full erection he raised up, spread her legs apart and poised himself above her. She lay like a corpse as he descended, sliding smoothly into her body. *This is ridiculous,* he thought. His body was leaden with fatigue and he doubted that he would even be able to come again. But because she was there beside him, desirable and available, some compulsion drove him to take her yet another time.

He set a gentle rhythm for himself, and Greta's body, asleep or not, was comfortable and accommodating. She seemed neither to enjoy nor resent what he was doing to her. For Faro there was a pleasure, quite distinct from the wrenching joy of climax, in simply feeling his organ sliding in and out of a woman's body. It was a succor of some strange variety.

He was surprised by the responses he eventually began to receive from deep within Greta's vagina. It felt as if the waves of some internal sea were washing gently over his manhood, caressing him with a soothing warmth. He began to come so smoothly that he was well into the experience before he realized what was taking place. Warm currents coursed through his body, draining away the last small quantity of energy which remained in him. He rolled to the side and his eyes sagged shut.

A small portion of both their lives slipped past them unawares.

"Faro?" Greta's voice was nearly as soft as the stillness of the night.

"Faro, was that a dream?" she asked. "Did you just make love to me?"

Her words failed to rouse him from his sleep, but it didn't matter. Within seconds she had joined him.

The rich smell of fresh coffee filled the bedroom, enticing Faro to wake up at last. Earlier he had been aware of Greta getting up and puttering around the room, but he had chosen not to rise just yet. Now though, as she wheeled the small serving cart to the edge of the bed and filled two china cups from the steaming silver pot, he opened his eyes and sat up.

"I thought you were going to sleep all day," Greta said. She was already dressed in a new pink gown with cascades of lace down the bodice and around the hem of the skirts. She had her hair arranged stylishly and she looked very pretty this morning.

"There are worse things to do with a day than to spend it in bed," Faro said. He added sugar and a measure of thick cream to the chicory coffee in his cup, then sampled its contents.

"And far better things as well, my dear," Greta said gaily. She picked up her cup and carried it into the adjoining bathroom. When she came out a moment later, she carried a small overnight case, which she set on the floor by the door. Faro noticed for the first time that all her luggage was packed and sitting there alongside his. After retrieving his valise and advantage tool case from the front desk the previous afternoon, he had never even bothered to unpack.

"What's all that about?" Faro asked. "Are we going somewhere?"

"I was serious about wanting to do some traveling," Greta said, "and I see no need to postpone it. When the *Hartford Cloud* leaves the docks in two hours heading for Jamaica, I intend to be on it. Have you ever been to Jamaica, Faro?"

"I can't say that I have," he told her. He drained his cup of lukewarm coffee and cream, then poured himself another from the pot. "Two hours, huh?" he asked.

"I sent one of the hotel people down to the ship to

make the arrangements," Greta told him. "And after Jamaica will come London, Paris, Rome . . . Isn't it all thrilling? It's the kind of trip I've dreamed about all of my life!"

Faro still found the prospect of staying in bed quite appealing. He thought he probably hadn't logged more than two or three hours of sleep the entire night, and he was still drowsy and tired. Another day there would be other ships heading for exotic places. He drank more coffee, hoping it would help him wake up.

"Isn't it wonderful how everything has turned out, Faro?" Greta asked brightly. She was puttering around the room, checking drawers and closets and making sure that none of her belongings would be left behind. "I am sorry about what happened to Anthony. But since it turned out that he was only out for himself all along, I suppose he's really responsible for what happened to him."

"I suppose," Faro said. He knew he should get up and start dressing. He sat for a moment staring at his clothes, which lay on a chair several feet away. The light in the room seemed to have a dusky tint to it this morning. He wondered if he might be hung over.

Greta disappeared into the sitting room for a moment, then came back to the doorway of the bedroom and stood staring at him. When Faro got up at last, his legs failed him unexpectedly and he toppled across the serving cart. Half a pot of steaming chickory splashed across the carpet, and his cup and saucer shattered as they hit the floor.

"What the hell?" Faro exclaimed in surprise. He looked up at Greta. She hadn't budged from the doorway. She seemed to be studying him. "What in the hell is going on here?" he growled. His tongue was beginning to feel like a thick foreign object in his mouth, and the objects in the room wouldn't quite be still.

"Whassa maaa w'me?" Faro slurred. Greta's image was beginning to blur and shimmer.

"You'd better get back on the bed, Faro," Greta advised him. "You can make it if you hurry. Otherwise you'll have to stay on the floor."

Faro reached up and clawed at the bedcovers, trying to pull himself up, but it took more strength than he had left in him. Finally he gave up and collapsed onto the carpet once more. "Whayougimme?" he rasped.

"It's some stuff one of the girls at Nell Garvin's had," Greta explained. "She said they used it to tame customers who got out of hand. I poured it in the coffee."

"Bish!" Even the mechanics of speaking were impossible to master. As Greta approached his side, she seemed to float through a cloud of dusky gray smoke.

"It just wouldn't have worked, Faro," she explained regretfully. "I want to be with a man, but I know it could never have been you. I'm sure that in a week or a month you would have left me, and I want something more than that. I am truly sorry about this, because I meant the things I told you last night. Being with you was a revelation to me. Making love with you brought me truly alive. But I knew all along that I never really mattered to you. You were only doing it because I was the one who was there."

Faro tried to respond, but he could not manage it. The knock-out drops were quickly taking control of him.

"I feel bad about the money side of things," Greta went on, "but this whole thing has been a gamble for all of us from the start, hasn't it? It just so happens that I came out the winner. To do all the things I want to do and go all the places I want to go, I'll need every cent of that hundred thousand dollars. But you're a resourceful fellow. Within a short time, I'm sure you'll be back on your feet again . . . both literally and figuratively." She chuckled lightly at her own joke.

Faro mustered all his remaining strength and reached out to grasp her ankle, but she knelt and parted his fingers as easily as if he was an infant. Then she leaned over and kissed his lips softly.

"Good-bye, Faro Blake," she whispered to him. "By the time you come to, I'll be out at sea. I hope someday you'll understand why I had to do this and that you'll forgive me for everything."

I will, he thought to himself, though he could not speak the words. He managed a faint smile. By the time she rose and started toward the door, consciousness was beginning to swirl away beyond his reach.

Chapter Nineteen

Faro sat by the window in the train compartment, watching the east Texas countryside sweep past outside. He liked this part of Texas best. With its forests, lakes and lively streams, it was not nearly so stark and forbidding as many other portions of the state.

A knock from the passageway outside interrupted his reverie, and he rose to open the door. "Ticket," the white-clad conductor announced. Faro produced his ticket from the pocket of his coat and handed it over to be punched.

"Going far?" the conductor asked.

"Quite a piece," Faro replied. "I've got my sights set on California."

"Well, have yourself a good trip," the conductor told him, "and don't let the wild red Indians steal your hair on the way."

"It's not likely, not anymore," Faro said. The

conductor handed back his ticket and moved on toward the next compartment. Faro closed the door and returned to his seat. In another two or three days he would pass through Denver and then ride on north to where he would change trains in Cheyenne. From there it would be a straight shot and a long ride on west to the Pacific Coast.

He withdrew a folded telegram from his pocket and read it once again, smiling to himself as his eyes lingered over the message:

> BEST NEWS OF MY LIFE STOP PROCEED WITH
> PURCHASE STOP WILL JOIN YOU SOON STOP
> NELL

And thus the future was determined. Faro had not experienced a single moment of regret since he wired Nell Garvin to meet him in San Francisco as soon as she could sell her place in Memphis.

After a while his mind turned to thoughts of Greta Wimbley. She was probably still at sea aboard the *Hartford Cloud,* on her way to Jamaica. The salt air and sunny climes would be good for her. Perhaps they might cleanse some of the bitterness from her spirit so that she could truly enjoy the new life on which she had embarked. But she would not find the exciting places she would soon be seeing quite so carefree as she expected. Faro was sure of that.

He put his suitcase up on the bed and opened it. Laying his spare shirts aside, he took a moment just to stare at the contents of the bottom of the valise. He could never recall having ever even seen that much money in one place, let alone possessing such an amount. One hundred and three thousand dollars! In the few days since he and Greta parted company he had counted it several times just for the hell of it.

What made it all so interesting was that it had been a gamble right up to the last minute who would finally end up with the money. Before she left the hotel, if Greta had thought to check the paper-wrapped package inside her suitcase, she would have seen that during the night Faro had switched her own bundles of newsprint for the real currency. Or if greed had not overwhelmed her and she had decided to leave him the five thousand dollars which was rightfully his, she would have discovered the switch. In either case, she could have easily found the real money where he hid it in the lining of the sofa beneath the cushions. Faro was unconscious at the time. He could not have stopped her, and she could have still boarded the sailing ship a wealthy woman instead of an unknowing pauper.

But that was not what happened. Reality had a way of transforming all the "what ifs" into trivialities.

That was life's gamble.